Andrea felt the first drops of rain hit her as she neared the lake. She was crying so hard, she stumbled and would have fallen if not for the boulder blocking her path. She dropped to her knees and wrapped her arms around her body.

A streak of lightening split the sky and Andrea was reminded of the night she arrived in this time. Maybe if she got struck by lightening, she would be sent back to her time.

"Please, God, take me home," she whispered. "Why are you doing this to me? Why am I here?" She leaned against the boulder and let the tears fall freely.

That's how Adam found her several minutes later. "Andrea," he said softly, kneeling down beside her.

She gazed at him through her tears. "Adam?" she whispered brokenly.

"Let's go home," he said, gently lifting her into his arms.

She didn't fight him as he carried her back to the house and up to her room. He sat her down on the side of the bed and began unbuttoning her shirt. She stopped him just as he reached the last one. "I'm not a liar," she whispered brokenly.

"I know," he returned, as he unbuttoned the last button and removed her wet shirt. The imploring look in her eyes was his undoing. He took her face between his hands and gently touched her lips with his.

"I should go," he breathed, ending the kiss.

As he turned, Andrea touched his arm. "Please, don't go," she whispered.

"If I stay, you know what will happen," he warned gently.

Judy Hinson

Timeless Love

A
Time
Travel Romance

By
Judy Hinson

Cover Design By: Lori Ramsey
of
TBI Designs.com

L & L Publishers

Judy Hinson

Published by:

L & L Publishers

L L Publishers.com
L.L.Publishers@sympatico.ca

145 Davis Trail
Thornton, Ontario
Canada
L0L 2N0

ISBN 0-9735534-6-4

Printed in the United States of America

Acknowledgments

It is with both love and gratitude that I wish to acknowledge and dedicate this book to my wonderful husband Art, my daughter Jamie, and my niece Carrie. Without their encouragement and faith, this book would not have been possible.

To my Mother and also my stepfather who passed before this book was published.

Special acknowledgements also go out to my two granddaughters who are the light of my life.

It is also with great pleasure to be able to recognize Lori Ramsey and Lisette Toth, for their assistance in the preparation of this book and for helping me pull it all together.

Judy Hinson

Prologue

Savannah, Georgia, March 2003

*S*ara jumped as a tree limb hit against her bedroom window. "I don't think we should be doing this Karen," she told her friend as they sat opposite each other on her bed.

"There's nothing to be afraid of," Karen chided. "It's only a game."

"I'm not afraid," Sara retorted. "It's just you know how my dad feels about me doing this sort of thing."

"Your dad isn't home, so how's he going to know?" Karen returned. "Come on, let's get started," she said excitedly, gently placing her fingers on the planchette.

Sara hesitantly placed her fingers as Karen had done and Karen began asking simple questions at first, about boys, how old she would be when she got married, how many kids she would have.

Sara began to relax and laugh along with Karen at the answers the board would give.

"Why don't we ask about your mother?" Karen suggested, quickly becoming bored with the inane questions. "Maybe the spirits will let us talk to her."

"Don't be ridiculous!" Sara scoffed. "You don't actually believe you can talk to dead people, do you?"

Karen shrugged. "Cassie and Linda said they talked to Linda's Aunt, and she told them things that had happened to her since her death."

"And you believed them?" Sara asked, shaking her head.

"Why not? Stranger things have happened," Karen replied. She placed her fingers back on the planchette. "Why don't we ask questions about your dad? Maybe we can find out if he's going to get married again. Is that okay with you?"

Sara agreed, knowing the answer to that question. Her father had sworn he would never marry again.

After her mother had died, her father had become bitter and refused to talk about her, so Sara assumed it was because he'd loved her so much that it was too painful.

Her thoughts were abruptly interrupted as she felt the planchette moving with great speed across the board. She just caught the last of Karen's question when the planchette started spelling out words.

"What did you ask it?" Sara gasped, as the planchette continued moving.

"I just wanted to know if we could speak to your mother," Karen whispered as she tried to catch the words the planchette was spelling out.

"What's it spelling?" Sara asked.

Karen grimaced as she tried to catch the letters. "Please, slow down!" she whispered. "D..a..n..g..e It's spelling the word 'danger'."

"Danger?" Sara repeated. "Why would it spell danger?"

"D..e..a..t" Suddenly, the planchette began moving faster and faster across the board, then went out of control and flew across the room. Both girls screamed as another loud crash sounded outside the window.

Sara quickly jumped off the bed and ran to the window just in time to see a bright streak of lightening hit the ground beyond the woods. A loud rumble followed. She turned to speak to Karen, but the room was empty.

"Karen?" she whispered. Obviously Karen had been so frightened by what had transpired she had fled.

Sara walked over and picked up the planchette and almost dropped it when she discovered it was hot. Frowning, she carefully placed it and the board back in its box and returned it to the closet where Karen had gotten it from earlier.

Shivering, she glanced out the window again, and then climbed into bed. Pulling the covers up to her chin, she reached over to turn the light out.

However, still somewhat shaken by what had occurred, she decided to leave the light on for a while.

Judy Hinson

Chapter 1

Savannah, Georgia, March 1889

*A*ndrea Marsh sat at the elaborate dining table, idly fingering the crystal glass she held in her hand as she tried to tune out the voices of her father and Nathan. It wasn't that the subject they were discussing was boring. On the contrary, it was the fact that she wasn't interested in anything Nathan Rivers had to say.

She often jumped at the chance to get any information she could on breeding horses, which was the conversation taking place, but she just didn't want to hear the sound of Nathan's voice.

She couldn't understand why her father continued his association with the man who sat across from her. As far as she was concerned, the two men had nothing in common. Her father was a soft-spoken, gentle man, who had worshiped her mother and adored her. Nathan on the other hand, was obnoxious, rude, and one of the most infuriating men she had ever met.

Oh he was handsome, with his black hair, which was beginning to gray at the temples, and his deep blue eyes. He stood well over six feet tall and carried himself with confidence. Andrea knew that women, young and old, chased after him, trying to win his heart and his money. However, she found him conceited and overbearing and when he looked at her with those cold blue eyes, all she felt was disgust.

Nathan had moved to Savannah two years ago from Canton, Ohio, and had purchased the only bank in town. Shortly after taking over the bank, he began foreclosing on the farms and ranches of families who were unable to keep up their mortgage payments. His latest purchase had been the Belmont Ranch, which adjoined theirs, and his pursuit of her had been constant ever since.

"Andrea," her father spoke softly, breaking into her thoughts.

"I'm sorry Father, what were you saying?"

"I was saying that Cynthia Graham's party this Saturday evening would be the perfect opportunity for us to make our announcement," Nathan responded before Jonathan could say anything.

Cynthia Graham was the daughter of William Graham, who was the only Judge in Chatham County, and was the most vain and bothersome woman Andrea has ever met. Cynthia was an attractive woman and had a lot of friends, but Andrea was not among them. It was for this reason that Andrea had no use for her and would never go to any party Cynthia was giving. So, why Nathan would even suggest they attend one of Cynthia's parties, was beyond Andrea.

Andrea glanced over at Saralyn, who sat at the other end of the table and noticed how her fork had stopped in midair on its way to her mouth.

Saralyn Flanders and Andrea Marsh were as different as night and day. Where Andrea was small and had a dark complexion, Saralyn was tall and very light skinned. Her hair was a strawberry blond and her eyes were light blue. Where Andrea lived outdoors most of her life around horses, Saralyn spent her days inside running her mother's home. But, no matter the differences between the two, they had been best friends since birth.

"What announcement?" Andrea asked, a coldness gripping her at the expression on her father's face.

"You didn't tell her?" Nathan glared at Jonathan.

"I haven't had an opportunity to do so yet," Jonathan replied quietly.

"I suppose I'll have to tell her," Nathan spat. He turned to Andrea and smiled.

"Your father has graciously agreed to accept my request for your hand in marriage and I've decided that Cynthia's party would be the perfect time to announce our engagement."

Andrea laughed, "Surely you jest."

"I don't joke about things this serious," Nathan responded.

"Then you will be announcing your engagement without me," Andrea stated coldly, shoving herself away from the table.

"It's all been arranged, Andrea," Nathan said quietly. "We will be married Easter Sunday."

Andrea stared at her father. "You arranged this without asking me first?" she hissed.

"It's for the best, Andrea," Jonathan responded quietly.

"Best for whom?" she asked, glaring at him. She threw her napkin down on the table and started toward the door.

"You might as well resign yourself to it, Andrea," Nathan called after her. "You will be my wife."

Andrea turned and gave him a look that immediately wiped the smug smile from his face. "It will be a cold day in hell before I marry you," she spat, and walked stiffly from the room.

Nathan rose to follow her, but Jonathan placed a hand out, stopping him. "Let her go," he said quietly. "She'll come around eventually."

"She'd better, old man, or you'll wish you'd never met me," Nathan returned coldly. He walked from the room and grabbing his coat and hat in the foyer, slammed out the front door.

"I already do," Jonathan muttered to himself.

"What have you done, Jonathan?" Saralyn, who had sat quietly listening, asked.

"It doesn't concern you, Saralyn," Jonathan replied quietly as he got up from the table and walked into the library. He poured himself a drink and sat down in one of the wing chairs near the hearth. He sighed as he ran a hand wearily across his eyes.

Saralyn followed close behind, refusing to accept his dismissal of her. "It does concern me, Andrea is like a sister to me and what affects her, affects me."

"I made a judgment call and that's the end of it," he told her curtly.

"And Andrea has to pay for your judgment call?" she laughed harshly. "I think what happened is that you got yourself in trouble at the gaming tables and now expect Andrea to clean up your mess."

"I gave my word and I do not plan to back down on it."

"You mean you gave Andrea's word," she spat. "I'm going up to see how she is," Saralyn told him coldly.

Jonathan sighed heavily. When had things begun to go wrong? A few months ago, everything was fine and he seemed to be in good spirits for the first time since his wife Claudia had died. The ranch was doing well and they were finally making money. What had possessed him to start drinking and gambling?

He thought back to his first meeting with Nathan at the gaming hall in town. He had sat down at one of the tables where a poker game was already in progress, and was introduced to Nathan. He had heard of Nathan, but had never met him.

The two of them had struck up a conversation and after that, they'd become friends, playing poker and drinking together at least three times a week.

He hadn't realized how far things had gone until the night he'd had a full house and knew no one else at the table could beat him. He had drank more than usual and felt confident he would walk away a winner.

The other two gentlemen at the table had folded, leaving the hand between him and Nathan. When Jonathan made his bet, Nathan met it and upped his bet. Jonathan had no more cash on him and asked Nathan to spot him. Nathan had smiled at him and told him he didn't do business that way but would make a wager.

Jonathan asked what he was proposing, and Nathan told him that if he won, his daughter, Andrea, would accept his proposal of marriage, and if Jonathan won, he would have his ranch free and clear and turn the title to the Belmont Ranch next to his over to him.

Jonathan was so sure he had the winning hand; he didn't hesitate in accepting the wager. He smiled when he laid his full house out on the table, kings over queens, and was reaching for his winnings when Nathan stopped him by producing four aces.

Astonished, Jonathan tried to reason with Nathan, asking him to give him time to pay off his debt, but Nathan refused. He wanted Andrea as his wife and nothing would change his mind.

Jonathan was certain Nathan had cheated, but had no way of proving it. So, being the honorable man he was, he accepted Nathan's proposal. Only he had never found the courage to tell Andrea and knew that after tonight, she would never forgive him.

Lightening split the sky as thunder rumbled outside, bringing Jonathan out of his musings. He had to try and explain to Andrea and beg her forgiveness.

"Andrea, may I come in?" Saralyn asked, knocking lightly on the door. At Andrea's response, Saralyn opened the door and went in. "Are you all right?" she asked.

"Did you hear what he said?" Andrea asked when Saralyn sat down on the bed beside her.

"I heard," Saralyn replied quietly. "What are you going to do?"

"Well, I'm certainly not going to marry Nathan Rivers." she replied. She flinched slightly when she heard her father calling her from downstairs.

"Maybe you should go and listen to what your father has to say," Saralyn suggested.

"I'll listen, but it won't change anything. I'm not going to marry Nathan."

"I'll wait here," Saralyn told her.

Jonathan stood at the bottom of the stairs and called for Andrea. After several attempts with no response, he decided to go upstairs. Just as he took the first step, she appeared at the top of the stairs. "Will you please come down?" he asked quietly. "We need to talk."

Andrea glanced around to see if Nathan was lurking in the shadows and not seeing him, proceeded to go down the stairs. She was still wearing the emerald green gown she had worn at dinner and the color brought out the flecks of green in her brown eyes. She was beautiful and every time Jonathan looked at her, he was reminded of his wife.

"I need to explain things to you," he said as she stopped in front of him.

"I would say so," she replied coolly.

"Can we go into the library and sit down?" he asked.

"I want to know why you took it upon yourself to commit me to marry Nathan, knowing full well how I feel about him," she said, ignoring his request.

"He really isn't that bad," Jonathan said. "He's handsome and very wealthy. You would never want for anything being his wife."

"I don't want for anything now," she said. "My life is fine just the way it is."

"It could be better," he argued. "What if something were to happen to me? What would you do?"

"I'm capable of taking care of myself, Father, and you very well know that."

Jonathan sighed. This was going to be harder than he thought. "You don't have any choice in the matter, Andrea," he said quietly.

"Of course I do," she stated. Narrowing her eyes, she watched the expressions play across her father's face. "What have you done?" she whispered, fear setting in. Not giving him time to respond, she answered for him. "You lost at the gaming tables, didn't you?"

Jonathan winced at her tone and tried to explain the events of that awful night, trying to avoid his daughter's eyes. He knew the disgust he would see there if he made direct contact with her. When he had finished, he reached inside his coat pocket and pulled out a handkerchief and wiped the moisture from his forehead.

"All you have to do is go to the bank and get the funds to pay Nathan what you owe him," Andrea said simply when he had finished.

"He won't accept any money," Jonathan said. "He wants you and if you refuse, he will foreclose on the ranch."

"He doesn't have the authority to do that!" Andrea cried.

"Yes, he does," Jonathan replied. "Nathan owns the bank that holds the mortgage on this ranch and he can foreclose any time he chooses."

"The bank can only foreclose on someone who is late on their payments," Andrea argued.

"Nathan has the power to do anything he wants, Andrea. That's what I've been trying to tell you. He has bought everything and everyone in this town."

"Well, he hasn't bought me and he never will," Andrea stated coldly. "I have no intention of ever marrying that man."

Jonathan jumped as a loud crash sounded outside. Andrea ignored him and the noise as she pushed past him and headed for the door. "Andrea, where are you going?" Jonathan asked.

"As far away from you as I can get," she snapped.

"Andrea, please," Jonathan begged, "it's beginning to storm and you shouldn't go out there." Andrea ignored his plea as she slammed out the door.

"Was that Andrea leaving?" Saralyn asked from the top of the stairs.

"Yes," Jonathan replied, sighing.

"Where is she going?"

"I don't know."

"Jonathan, it's beginning to storm. Andrea shouldn't be out there," she said, concern etching her voice.

"What do you want me to do, go after her?" He shook his head. "She'll be back as soon as she calms down. Why don't' you go on to bed."

"If it's all the same to you, I'll wait down here," she stated curtly as she walked past him into the library.

Andrea headed in the direction of the woods where she always went when she was upset or needed to think. The trees surrounding the area always made her feel peaceful.

She reached the woods and continued walking, not paying any attention to where she was going. Soon, she had reached the outer edges and stopped to stare morosely out over the valley. It wasn't quite dusk yet, but the gathering dark clouds made it hard to see.

Anger at what her father had done coiled through her stomach and left her with a cold, hollow feeling. To keep the tears from falling, she drew in a long, deep breath, held it for several seconds then slowly released it.

Why had he done this, knowing how important the ranch was to her? What had possessed him to make any kind of agreement with Nathan? Didn't he realize what kind of man he was? Surely, her father had not been so drunk that he would auction her off like some animal?

The sharp, bitter cold wind rustled through the tall trees overhead and drew her attention. A slight chill cut through her lightweight gown and she hugged her arms around her shoulders.

Brief flashes of lightening illuminated the sky as she stood and gazed out across the land, her land.

Suddenly, another bolt of lightening gave a deafening crack. Startled, she screamed. Clasping her hands against her chest, she sucked in several quick breaths before turning to run back towards the house.

Suddenly, the sky opened up and huge torrents of rain came down. Shivering from the sudden cold, Andrea began to run in what she thought was the direction of home. She had only taken a few steps when she stumbled. Trying to right herself and continue, the hem of her gown caught on the bottom of her shoe and she let out a scream as she went flying.

***

Jonathan followed Saralyn into the library and walked straight over to the liquor cabinet and poured himself another portion of bourbon. Not saying a word to her, he began pacing in front of the fireplace, brooding over what had transpired between him and his daughter. Nothing was going right, and there would be hell to pay if Andrea did not go along with Nathan's plans of marriage.

An hour later and two more portions of bourbon, Jonathan decided not to wait up for Andrea.

"I'm going to bed," he announced.

"You're not going to wait for Andrea?" Saralyn asked, surprised.

"She's angry with me and most likely is punishing me by staying away. She'll return when she has cooled off."

"Are you sure?"

"Yes, I'm sure," he replied. "She's probably down at the stables letting steam off by talking to her horses. She'll be back, so you might as well go on up to bed too."

Saralyn hesitated, and then said, "All right, but I'm sure I won't sleep a wink until Andrea returns." She bade Jonathan goodnight and went upstairs.

Sighing, Jonathan finished off his drink and followed Saralyn up the stairs. Removing his clothes, he crawled into bed. Within minutes, he was fast asleep.

***

When he entered the dining room the next morning, Jonathan expected to see Andrea already seated at the table. Not finding her there, he decided to wait a few minutes before having Mattie serve breakfast.

After several minutes had passed and she still had not appeared, he asked Mattie go ahead and serve him. He was sure Andrea was still mad and her way of punishing him was to ignore him.

Saralyn entered with a frown on her face." Where's Andrea?" she asked.

"I suppose she's still abed," Jonathan replied.

Saralyn shook her head. "I knocked on her door, but got no response."

"She probably came in late last night and is still sleeping. Why don't you sit down and have breakfast. I'm sure Andrea will be down soon."

Before Saralyn could respond, Nathan entered. Jonathan sighed, not looking forward to what this visit would entail. "Would you like some breakfast?" he asked Nathan.

"Where's Andrea?" Nathan returned, ignoring Jonathan's offer.

"She hasn't come down yet," Jonathan replied.

"We need to get this matter settled, now," Nathan said.

"It's not going to be as easy as you think, Nathan," Jonathan said quietly. "Andrea is a very head strong young woman, and no one has *ever* made her do anything she didn't want to do."

"She'll go along with this if she doesn't want you to lose this ranch," Nathan stated coldly. "Send someone upstairs to bring her down," he ordered.

Jonathan sighed, shaking his head as he called Mattie into the room. "Mattie, would you please go up and tell Andrea that we are awaiting breakfast for her?" Mattie bobbed her head and left the room.

After Mattie left, he turned to Nathan. "You actually believe you can make a marriage work with someone who despises you?" he asked quietly.

Nathan glared at him. "Once she's married to me and sees what I can offer her, she won't remember why she dislikes me."

Jonathan arched his eyebrows at how Nathan used the word 'dislikes' instead of 'despises'. Before he could comment, Mattie came back in.

"She ain't in her room, Mr. Marsh," she said. "And it looks like Ms. Andrea ain't slept in her bed all night."

"That's impossible," Jonathan said, heading for the stairs, with Saralyn and Nathan following. "I'm sure I heard her come back in last night."

"Come back in from where?" Nathan asked.

When they entered Andrea's bedchamber, Jonathan realized Mattie had spoken the truth. Andrea's bed had not been slept in. Surely she didn't spend the entire night in the stables?

"Where is she?" Nathan demanded.

"I don't know," Jonathan replied. "We had a few words after you left last night, and she ran out of the house. It was storming and I asked her not to go, but she wouldn't listen. I assume she spent the night in the stable."

Nathan strode from the room, taking the stairs two at a time. Jonathan and Saralyn followed, though not as quickly.

"Saralyn, you wait here in case Andrea returns," Jonathan suggested as she started to follow them. Saralyn nodded as she walked into the library.

When Jonathan and Nathan reached the stables, Andrea was nowhere in sight.

Jonathan asked Benji, the stable boy, if he had seen her last night or this morning.

"Ain't seen Ms. Andrea since yesterday morning," Benji replied. "Is Ms. Andrea missing?"

"No, she's not missing," Nathan responded harshly. He turned to Jonathan with a scowl on his face. "Where else would she go?"

Jonathan shook his head. "She doesn't have any friends close by, so I don't know where she would have gone."

"She mighta went out to the woods. She likes to walk out there sometimes," Benji offered quietly behind them.

"Seems your stable boy knows your daughter better than you do," Nathan stated dryly as he headed in the direction of the woods.

When they reached the woods, Nathan started calling her name. Jonathan looked around, hoping to find some clue as to whether she had been there or not.

"She's not here," Nathan said flatly. "Is this something the two of you planned?" He asked Jonathan accusingly. "If it is, you can just forget it. Andrea and I will be married no matter what either of you want."

Jonathan made no response as he continued through the woods. When he came to the clearing beyond, he started calling out Andrea's name. Nathan followed and stood beside him.

When there was no response, Nathan turned and headed back in the direction of the house. Jonathan followed but stopped when something behind one of the trees caught his attention.

Moving closer, he recognized the item as one of the slippers Andrea had been wearing the night before. He glanced around; afraid he might find her among the bushes or trees. He released a sigh of relief when he did not see her body lying anywhere around.

Why would her slipper be here, he wondered? Had she tripped and somehow lost it? Where was she? Was she angry enough with him to pull a disappearing act? Was she at this moment hiding somewhere, hoping her disappearance would somehow make him change his mind about his plans for her? No matter what stunt she was pulling, when she came out of hiding, she would have to marry Nathan and there was nothing either one of them could do about it.

"Did you find her?" Saralyn demanded when Jonathan entered the house.

"No," he replied. "There was no sign of her anywhere."

"Are you telling me she just disappeared?"

"I don't know what I'm telling you!" Jonathan snapped. At the pained expression on her face, he said, "I'm sorry, Saralyn. I'm sure Andrea is just hiding somewhere."

"How can you be so sure?" she asked worriedly.

"Because I know Andrea, and she's just doing this because she's angry with me. She'll return soon, I'm sure."

Saralyn wasn't as sure as Jonathan, but she would give him the benefit of the doubt. She knew how angry

Andrea was last night, but didn't believe she would do something this horrible.

"Where's Nathan?" she asked.

"He's probably still out searching."

She sat down in the wing chair near the hearth and watched as Jonathan paced back and forth, waiting for his daughter to come home.

Chapter 2

*T*he storm had finally passed so Sara and Daniel quickly finished their breakfast and headed for the lake. She had promised him yesterday that they would go fishing today, if the weather permitted it.

"Do you think Dad will take us to the fair this year?" Daniel asked as he placed a sleek brown worm on his hook.

"Probably not," Sara replied. "We didn't go last year, so we most likely won't go this year."

Daniel shrugged. "I guess I was just hoping."

"I know," Sara said quietly. She felt sorry for Daniel and tried to spend as much time with him as she could. She knew he missed their father and since their mother had died a little over a year ago, Adam hardly had time for his children anymore.

She hated the way things were lately. The only time they seemed to spend with their father was at dinner. He spent his days in his office in town and most of his nights with his friend, Carol. There were times she wished she could tell him how she felt, especially about his neglect of Daniel, but knew it would do no good. Adam's response to anything she and Daniel did was met with silence or punishment.

Daniel was at the age where he needed a man's guidance. However, the raising of him was left up to Sara and their housekeeper, Mrs. Floyd. Sara hoped

26

that her father would see what was happening before it was too late.

"Let's go see if we can find any deer tracks in the woods," Daniel suggested, lying his pole down. Sara agreed as she laid her pole down beside his and followed him into the woods.

"Did you hear that?" Daniel asked, stopping as they came to the clearing past the woods.

"Hear what?" she returned.

"Listen," he whispered.

Sara frowned. "I don't hear anything, Daniel."

"There it is again!" Daniel exclaimed, pointing in the direction of the cliff. "It sounds like moaning."

Sara cocked her head in the direction Daniel was pointing when suddenly she too heard a sound. "Let's go check it out," she told him.

"What do you think it is?" Daniel asked following close behind his sister as she made her way near the cliff.

"We won't know until we get there," she replied.

"What if it's a wild animal or an escaped convict?"

"From the sound of the moaning, I don't think whatever it is will be of any danger to us right now," she assured him.

As they neared an area with tall trees and brush, Sara spotted something green. As another moan came from that area, she realized the green she had spotted was a shoe.

Both she and Daniel were surprised when they found a woman lying under a tree, her clothes covered in mud and bleeding from a cut on her forehead.

Sara bent down and lightly touched the woman's forehead. The woman's eyes popped open at the light touch and frightened, she pushed it away.

"I was just checking to see how bad you were cut," Sara said. Andrea frowned, but didn't respond. "What are you doing here?" Sara asked as she stood back up.

A feeling of foreboding settled over Sara as an image of her and Karen playing with the Quija board last night.

"Wow! Look how's she's dressed!" Daniel exclaimed, pointing to the dress the woman was wearing.

"Where am I?" the woman whispered, as she tried to focus her eyes.

"Who are you and how did you get here?" Sara asked instead.

Andrea looked up at the girl who couldn't have been much more than eleven or twelve years old. She had dark brown hair, which was pulled back and tied with a ribbon, and her eyes were a dark hazel. The boy, who kept watching her warily, looked to be about eight or nine years old and had hair the color of charcoal and eyes so dark blue that they were almost black.

"My name is Andrea and I'm not sure how I got here," she replied, looking around. The last thing she remembered was tripping over something and flying through the air just before darkness descended and wrapped her in oblivion. She tried to sit up but moaned as pain shot through her head.

Get up, her brain commanded, and for the first time in her life, she felt removed from her body. It was as though her body wasn't hers. Was this death, this separation from her body?

Then the images came to her… arguing with her father… being in a storm. Shaking her head in confusion, she focused on what the girl was saying to her.

"I think you'd better lie still," Sara suggested. "That looks like a pretty nasty cut on your forehead."

Andrea gingerly touched her forehead. "I'll be all right in a minute."

"Are you sure?" Sara asked worriedly.

Andrea noticed the girl staring at her with a peculiar expression on her face. "What's wrong?" she asked.

"I was just wondering why you're dressed like that," Sara replied, pointing to Andrea's dress.

Andrea looked down at her clothes. Her emerald gown was covered with mud and torn in several places. Her father was going to be very angry when he saw this. The material for this gown cost a fortune and he had paid Mrs. Beal, her seamstress, more than her usual amount to make the gown for her.

All of Andrea's gowns were specially made for her, but this one was her favorite. It had long sleeves coming to a V at her wrists with tiny pearls surrounding the cuffs, cut low just above the breast and tapered at the waist. The emerald color brought out the green flecks in her eyes.

"I suppose it is a little dressy for this time of day," She tried sitting up again and managed to make it with help from Sara. "I didn't get a chance to change before I left the house last night," she added.

Sara frowned. "Were you having a masquerade party?" she asked.

"A what?" Andrea returned, also frowning.

"Never mind. Can you stand?"

"I think so," Sharp pain radiated through her head as she came slowly to her feet. She looked around, searching for something more familiar. "If you will help me, I'm sure I can find my way home."

"Where do you live?" Sara asked, taking Andrea's elbow to help steady her.

"On the other side of the woods," she replied.

"You don't live there," Daniel stated gruffly, coming to stand beside his sister. "That's where we live."

"I'm sure that is where I live," Andrea said, looking sharply at the young man.

Sara motioned for Daniel to be quiet. Evidently the lady had hit her head harder than she thought. "What's the matter?" she asked when Andrea came to a sudden halt.

"Something is wrong," Andrea whispered as they came out on the other side of the woods.

"What do you mean?"

"I'm not sure," she whispered, looking around her. This must be the Belmont property, she thought to herself. She must have gotten turned around last night and ended up here.

Taking her elbow again, Sara began walking.

Andrea froze as they came to what looked to be a road covered with something black. Sticking out of the ground was a pole with some sort of box with letters on it that spelled the name Rivers.

"Who are you?" she whispered, looking sharply at the young girl standing beside her.

"I'm Sara and this is my brother, Daniel."

"What is your sir name?"

"You mean my last name?" Sara asked, giving her a strange look. Andrea nodded. "It's Rivers," she replied.

Andrea gasped. Were these two children related to Nathan? And if so, what were they doing here?

"What's wrong with her?" Daniel asked.

"Sh!" Sara whispered, giving Daniel a sharp glance.

"Are you coming?" Sara asked Andrea. "We really need to get that cut on your head looked at."

Andrea allowed Sara to lead her up the long drive to the front of the house, and came to another sudden stop as she stared at what looked like her home.

The house was white with columns surrounding the front porch, like hers. It was a two story Colonial style with dark blue shutters on the windows. Where the front of her house was covered in cobblestone, this one was covered in blades of grass. More confused than ever, she glanced around her.

Andrea stiffened when her eyes came in contact with several types of machinery. "What are those?" she asked in a raspy voice.

Turning to look at her shocked expression, Sara said, "Cars. You know, vehicles of transportation."

"What powers such...such things?" Her expression remained incredulous.

"Gasoline: oil, from under the earth."

"You actually get in one of those things?"

Sara frowned. This woman must have really knocked some screws loose, she thought, if she didn't even remember what a car was. "It's the only way to get anywhere."

Andrea shook her head as the girl named Sara opened the front door and led her inside. She then told Daniel to go get someone as she led Andrea into what appeared to be the parlor.

Andrea could do nothing but stare at the room as she sank into the chair that Sara stood her in front of. This definitely was not her parlor. The furniture was designed like none she had ever seen before, not like the Colonial style in her parlor, nor were the paintings on the walls anything like the ones that hung on hers.

"Can I get you something to drink?" the girl asked, concern etching her features at the frightened expression on Andrea's face.

"No," Andrea replied vaguely, continuing to stare at her surroundings.

"Don't worry, Mrs. Floyd will have you fixed up in no time and then you can go home," Sara assured her, trying to ease her fear.

Home? If the little boy was right and this wasn't her home, then where was it? Andrea wondered silently. She knew last night she had been in the woods when the storm suddenly hit and she had tripped and that was the last thing she remembered. When she woke up this morning, she was in strange, but somewhat familiar surroundings.

A couple of minutes later, a short, heavyset woman with gray hair and brown eyes came into the room. Andrea assumed she was these children's grandmother. However, she found out shortly that was not a correct assumption.

"Daniel said we have an injured woman in here," Mrs. Floyd said. Her eyebrows rose slightly when she caught sight of the woman's apparel. "He said you fell and hit your head," she said, smiling.

Andrea gingerly touched her head. "I think it's okay now."

"Let me have a look," Mrs. Floyd said.

"Can you tell me where I am?" Andrea asked, "It seems I somehow wondered off last night and got lost."

"This is Mr. Rivers' house," Mrs. Floyd replied. "My name is Catherine and I'm the housekeeper here." She pulled the hair away from Andrea's forehead and grimaced as she looked at the cut that was already beginning to turn a deep shade of purple.

Andrea watched her warily as she took a small bottle from a box she had and then pour some sort of dark red liquid onto a cloth she held in her hand. She winced slightly as the woman touched the cold cloth to her forehead. She didn't know what the woman was using, but it burned and smelled awful. After she had cleansed the wound, Mrs. Floyd took something else out of the box and started to place it on her forehead. Andrea frowned, thinking it must be some kind of bandage.

"You're all set," Mrs. Floyd said as she put the bottle back in the box and closed it. "You're probably going to experience some dizziness and disorientation for awhile, so would you like someone to drive you home?"

"Home?" Andrea repeated. "I'm not sure I know where that is at the moment."

Mrs. Floyd eyed her skeptically. "You don't remember where you live?"

"No," Andrea replied honestly.

"Do you remember anything at all?"

"I remember going for a walk through the woods last night and it beginning to rain."

Mrs. Floyd nodded her head. "That was a really bad storm we had last night."

"And I remember starting back home when I tripped over something and fell. The next thing I remember is waking up to these two children standing over me," she pointed a finger at Sara and Daniel. She saw the pity in Mrs. Floyd's eyes and stiffened slightly as she straightened up.

"Well, don't you worry about a thing," Mrs. Floyd said, gently patting her hand. "We'll get you home. What's your name, child?"

"Andrea Marsh," she replied. "My father and I have a plantation around here. It's called Briarcliff. Have you heard of it?"

"Don't think I have," Mrs. Floyd replied, shaking her head, sure she had never heard of any actual plantations still standing in this area. She knew there were still a couple of them on the outskirts of town, but didn't know who owned them.

"No matter. We'll find out where it is and someone will drive you home." She turned to Sara. "Honey, why don't you take Ms. Marsh upstairs and let her freshen up a bit. I'll start calling around and see if anyone knows where this Briarcliff place is."

The woman's use of words puzzled Andrea. What did she mean by calling around? Did she mean she would go from plantation to plantation asking people if they knew her? She didn't question Mrs. Floyd as she stood and followed Sara from the room.

"And Sara honey, see if you can find something a little more clean for Ms. Marsh to change into." Mrs. Floyd suggested.

Andrea followed Sara up the stairs and down a long hallway, frowning at the strange paintings that hung on the walls. At the end, she was ushered into a room that was decorated in soft green and light beige, which gave the room a sunny appearance.

"The bathroom is right through that door," Sara told her, pointing to an opening next to a big brass bed that stood against the wall. "I'll go see if I can find you something to wear." She left the room without waiting for a reply.

Andrea stood in the middle of the room, a feeling of unease settling over her. She walked over to a desk that stood in one corner of the room and started going through some of the drawers. She froze as her eyes fell on a piece of paper that looked to be part of a newspaper. In bold letters across the top, the words, 'Savannah Morning News' was printed on it, and it was dated March 14, 2003. Surely this was some kind of joke! She couldn't possibly have traveled over one hundred years into the future!

She walked over to the bed and slowly sank down on it. Something was definitely wrong here. She knew she had to be dreaming and prayed she would wake up soon and be back in her own bed.

She had no idea how long she had been sitting on the bed when she decided to get up and go into the room Sara had told her was a "bathroom", whatever that was.

There were a lot of strange things in this room. Something attached to the floor in one corner, which was made of marble and against the wall facing the marble structure was a cabinet with a spout attached to the top of it. She walked over to it and reached down and slowly turned one of the handles and to her surprise, a stream of water shot out of it. "Amazing!" she whispered, turning the handle back and forth.

Stepping back, her shoulder hit something on the wall. Turning, she gazed sharply at the small thing protruding from the wall. It had tiny buttons on it with two knobs in the lower right hand corner. She reached out to touch it when suddenly she heard voices. Startled, she jumped back and looked around the small room. There was no one else with her, so where had the voices come from? Curious, she moved closer to the box and reaching out, touched one of the knobs and slowly turned it to the right. The voices grew louder and she realized they were coming from within the box. How was that possible? She wondered.

Just as she started to turn the knob back to the left, she heard her name spoken. She stood transfixed in the middle of the tiny room and listened as the boy Daniel and Ms. Floyd talked about her.

"She's a strange lady, don't you think, Mrs. Floyd?" Daniel was saying.

"Why do you say that, Daniel?" Mrs. Floyd returned.

"Look at the way she's dressed, and some of the things she said were pretty weird."

"What sort of things?"

"She kept saying she lived here."

"Maybe she was just confused."

"Know what I think?" Daniel asked.

"No, but I'm sure you'll tell me," she said, laughing softly.

"I think she escaped from one of those crazy hospitals."

"I don't think so, Daniel. I think Ms. Marsh just got lost last night and is a bit confused."

"But look at the way she's dressed!"

"Maybe she was at a party," Mrs. Floyd suggested.

"Uh-uh," he said, shaking his head. "Sara asked her about that and she said she hadn't been to any party. Sara thinks she might have gotten drunk or was high on drugs and got lost in the woods."

"Why don't you let me worry about Ms. Marsh," Mrs. Floyd told him. "As soon as she's feeling better, we'll see about getting her home."

"I think we oughta call the police," Daniel said.

"If your dad thinks the police need to be called, he'll call them," she said sharply. "Now, why don't you go on outside and I'll call you when dinner is ready."

"Do I have to?"

She nodded. "It won't be long, I promise."

"Oh, all right," he mumbled.

When the box became silent, Andrea wiped the tears from her eyes and reached over and turned the knob back to the left. So, the little boy thought she was crazy. Perhaps if she told them what she really thought, they would be more inclined to help her. On the other hand, maybe they wouldn't believe her and think she *was* crazy.

She took one of the cloths hanging on a hook on the wall and turned the spout on. Cupping her hands under the stream of water, she splashed her face several times then gently dried it with the cloth.

She walked back into the bedchamber and found Sara standing there holding a pair of trousers and a shirt. "I've brought these for you to wear until you get home," Sara said, handing her the clothes. "They've been packed away for some time, so they might be a little wrinkled." Andrea did not respond as she took them from her. "Are you all right?"

Andrea drew in a deep steadying breath, trying to gain control of her tumbling emotions. Should she tell this young girl what she thought might have happened to her? Would she believe her or would she be like her brother? She looked deeply into Sara's eyes and seeing a small spark of compassion, decided to trust her.

"Sara, there's something I need to tell you," she began hesitantly. "I fear my story may seem strange to you, but I have no one else to turn to. I need to trust someone. Can I trust you?" Sara nodded her head slowly as she waited for Andrea to continue. "I'm not sure how or why this happened, but when I woke up this morning I was here, when last night as the storm began, I was at my house."

She placed the clothes on the bed and turned to face Sara. "Can you tell me what the date is?" she asked.

"March fourteen," Sara replied.

"What year?"

Sara frowned. "Two Thousand Three," Sara replied, frowning.

Suddenly, Andrea's heart twisted, causing a sharp, cutting pain to pierce her chest. Her whole body felt weak as she sank down on the bed. "Are you sure?" she whispered, turning her troubled gaze to Sara.

"Of course I'm sure," Sara replied. "I can show you a calendar if you'd like."

Aware of her baffled expression that she spoke the truth, Andrea's insides coiled tighter, making it hard for her to breathe. "That won't be necessary," she whispered. As impossible as it seemed, she had somehow been thrown into the future during the storm last night.

"Would you please explain what's going on?" Sara asked.

Andrea took a deep breath and slowly released it. "Last night when it began to storm, I started running back to my home and tripped. When I fell, I must have hit my head, I don't really remember, but when I woke up this morning, I was here."

"That much we already know," Sara said, pointing to the bandage on her forehead. "You have a cut on your forehead to prove that."

"What I'm trying to say is that when I tripped and obviously hit my head, I was in the year eighteen hundred eighty-nine, not two thousand three." She watched the play of emotions cross Sara's face and waited for what she had told her, to sink in.

"You're saying you traveled through time?" Sara asked with uncertainty in her voice.

"Yes," Andrea whispered, taking hold of Sara's small hand. "Think about it. Does this gown look like anything from your time? No. This gown was specially made for me by a seamstress with material that was shipped from France. I have dozens of gowns just like this one."

"You could have been at a party," Sara said, still uncertain.

Andrea shook her head. "I already told you I wasn't at any party, Sara. Last night my father and I argued and I became so enraged, I ran from my home. I had no idea the storm would be as bad as it was and when the rain began to come down hard, I began running back, only I didn't make it."

"I don't know," Sara said. "It sounds too crazy to me."

Andrea winced, remembering Daniel's words to Mrs. Floyd. "I'm not crazy, Sara," she whispered. "I don't even know what that thing is that has water coming out of it is," she said, pointing to the bathroom.

"You mean the sink?" Sara asked, frowning.

"I guess," Andrea replied, frowning. "We don't have those where I come from. We have a well outside that we have to pump water from to take inside. Your world is foreign to me, Sara."

Sara turned her head and saw fear in her expression. "You don't have a bathroom?" Sara asked, surprised.

"No," Andrea replied. "And, what is that square box with the glass doors?" she asked.

"Box..."she said, frowning. "Oh, you mean the shower."

"What is a shower?"

"It's like a bathtub, only you stand in it and hot and cold water runs down your body. It's better than taking a bath," she explained.

"You don't have to heat the water?" Andrea whispered.

Sara smiled slightly. "No, the cold water is stored in a water heater and when you turn on the water, the water heater heats it up and by the time it gets to the shower, it's hot."

Andrea shook her head. "I have never heard of such a thing. And, what is that oval shaped thing attached to the floor that has a top on it?"

Sara frowned, and then suddenly grinned. "Oh, that's the toilet."

"What is a toilet?"

"It's where...you know, where you go to the bathroom." At Andrea's confusion, she said, "It's where you go to relieve yourself."

The look on Andrea's face was so hilarious, Sara couldn't help but giggle.

"You mean you don't use chamber pots?" Andrea asked.

Sara's laughter died and a frown creased her brow at the serious look on Andrea's face.

Andrea suddenly felt a tiny bit of hope that maybe Sara was beginning to believe her. "You're beginning to believe what I've been telling you, aren't you?" she asked quietly.

"I don't know what to believe," Sara replied exasperated. She reached down and picked up the clothes from the bed and handed them back to Andrea. "I should go so you can change. I'll ask Mrs. Floyd if she's been able to contact your family."

"Mrs. Floyd won't find anyone related to me in this time, Sara," Andrea said softly, her hopes dashed.

"Sara," she said, halting the girl at the door. "Could you get the back of my dress for me? I can't reach the buttons."

Sara hesitated momentarily, then walked back over and unbuttoned the tiny pearl buttons at the back of Andrea's dress. When she had finished, she left, closing the door behind her.

The tears coursed down Andrea's cheeks as she slowly removed her gown. There had to be a way to convince Sara that she was telling the truth, but how?

She thought about her father and Saralyn possibly searching frantically for her. Did they think she had been so angry that she could have run away?

She grimaced at the clothes Sara had left for her, as they appeared to be men's clothing. When she had finished changing, she walked over to the dresser and picked up the comb that was lying on top of it and began pulling the tangles from her hair. The comb froze in mid air as her eyes caught sight of a miniature painting that was sitting on top of the dresser. That's it! These people must have other paintings somewhere, and since their sir name was Rivers, they might be related to Nathan. And if that were the case, surely they had at least one painting of him. And if they did, Sara would have to believe her then.

Chapter 3

 ndrea found Sara in the kitchen with Mrs. Floyd. She was almost afraid to enter when she saw all the strange machines standing against the walls. She braced herself and hesitantly entered the room.

"Thank you for the clothes," she said quietly to Mrs. Floyd.

"You're welcome," Mrs. Floyd responded, turning to give her a smile.

"I also appreciate you taking care of my injury," Andrea said as she sat down at the table across from where Sara sat peeling and cutting potatoes.

"I haven't been able to locate your family yet, but I'm sure we will," Mrs. Floyd informed her. "So, in the meantime, you can stay and have dinner with us if you'd like."

"I would like that, thank you." She glanced over at Sara. "I noticed all the paintings you have hanging on the wall along the stairs," she spoke to Sara, who had not looked at her yet.

"Those are Mr. Rivers' ancestors," Mrs. Floyd replied. "His family can be traced back to the eighteen hundreds."

"Really," Andrea murmured, watching Sara closely.

"I believe he still has some old pictures stored in boxes up in the attic."

"Why would you want to look at old pictures?" Sara asked stiffly, finally looking at Andrea.

"I love looking at old pictures," Andrea replied softly.

"Sara, why don't you take Ms. Marsh up to the attic and see what you can find," Mrs. Floyd suggested.

"What about the potatoes?"

"I'll finish them. You two go on and see what you can find."

"Just what are you up to?" Sara whispered as they left the kitchen. "Why do you want to look at old pictures?"

Andrea shrugged but made no response, instead asked, "What are all those machines in the kitchen?"

"They're appliances," Sara replied. At the confused expression on her face, Sara sighed, "You know, refrigerator, stove, microwave."

"I know what a stove is, but what is a refrig…what did you call it?"

"A refrigerator; it's where food is kept to keep it cold."

"Oh, you mean an ice box."

"Yea, I guess so," Sara said, frowning.

"And what is a micro wave?"

"It's what you heat food in."

"But, isn't that what a stove is for?"

"A microwave is faster than a stove. You can cook in it quicker and heat leftovers and stuff."

Andrea made no further comment as Sara opened the door to the attic and went inside. Andrea followed and watched as Sara pulled one box down from the shelf and handed it to her, then pulled another one down and placed it on the floor.

"Are there any pictures of your great, great grandfather in any of these boxes?" Andrea inquired, opening the first box.

"I really don't know what pictures are in these boxes," Sara replied.

"Do you know what his name was?"

"His name was Nathan Randolph Rivers," Sara replied as a feeling of dread started to settle over her. She sat down on one of the crates behind Andrea and watched curiously as she rummaged through the pictures.

"Oh my God!" Andrea gasped, staring at the small painting she held in her hand.

"What?" Sara asked, hesitantly moving to stand next to her.

"Is this your great, great grandfather?" Andrea asked, her hand shaking as she handed Sara the painting.

"This picture is old and worn and you can hardly see his face, but it could be him."

Andrea was going through the box again when another small gasp escaped from her lips.

"What now?" Sara groaned.

Andrea's hand shook as she handed the painting to Sara. "It's me," she whispered.

The blood drained from Sara's face as she stared at the woman in the painting. It was very small and very old, but there was no denying that it could be Andrea. When she turned it over, her worst fears were realized when she read the date on the back.

"Do you believe me now?" Andrea whispered.

"This could be someone who just looks like you," Sara argued.

Andrea groaned. "Look at it, Sara. This is me!"

"I don't know what to believe!" Sara cried, throwing the picture back in the box. "We need to get back downstairs. Dad will be home soon."

"Okay," Andrea said, not wanting to upset her any further. "But will you at least keep an open mind about this and at least consider the possibility that I'm telling the truth?"

"It's too frightening to even consider such a thing," Sara whispered.

"I know," Andrea agreed. "If you're frightened by this, just imagine how I feel. I'm the one who got thrown into the future."

"I think I hear Dad," Sara said. "Come on. He'll be ready to sit down to dinner soon."

"Sara, what will happen when no one can locate my family?" Andrea asked quietly.

"Dad knows a lot of people. He'll be able to find someone who knows you," she said, still trying to convince herself that what Andrea said was not true.

"He won't find anyone here that knows me, Sara," she said. "There was just my father and me and now that I'm gone, there's no one to carry on the Marsh family line."

Before Sara could respond, Daniel burst through the door with a sour expression on his face. "Dad's home and he brought *Carol* with him."

Sara stiffened slightly. "We'd better get back downstairs."

"Mrs. Floyd is telling him about *her* right now," Daniel said, glaring at Andrea.

Andrea followed them from the attic, wondering at Daniel's attitude towards this person named Carol, not to mention his attitude towards her.

The two people in the dining room became silent when Andrea and the children entered.

Andrea braced herself for the questions she knew would be asked.

She released a shocked gasp when she caught sight of the man standing at the end of the table. She grasped the doorframe as a wave of dizziness came over her.

"Are you all right?" Sara whispered, taking her elbow to help steady her.

"Yes," Andrea replied shakily. She couldn't stop staring at the man she assumed was the father of these two children. He bore a strong resemblance to Nathan. However, he was taller and broader through the shoulders and his facial features were more pronounced, but there was no mistaking that he and Nathan were related to each other. His hair was black, like Nathan's, and his eyes were deep blue. However, where Nathan's eyes were cold, this man's were warm and friendly. He appeared to be about the same age as Nathan, who was in his middle thirties.

"So, you're Andrea," the man said, coming to stand in front of her. "I'm Adam Rivers and this is Carol Masters," he indicated the woman standing at the end of the table. "Catherine was just telling us what happened to you. I'm sure I can be of assistance in helping you find your family."

"Yes, Catherine was telling us about your accident," the woman named Carol said, moving to stand next to Adam. "Is it true that Sara and Daniel found you unconscious in the woods and that you have no memory of how you got there?"

Carol Masters was a very beautiful woman. The top of her head was even with Mr. Rivers' shoulders and her hair, which was shorter than any woman Andrea had ever seen, was a golden blond. And her eyes, which were now focused on Andrea, were a pale blue.

"Yes ma'am," Andrea replied, noting with satisfaction the stiffening of Carol's spine when she referred to her as "ma'am".

"Why don't we sit down," Adam suggested as he pulled out a chair for Andrea. He then pulled out Carol's chair then took his seat at the end of the table.

Andrea was amazed at the simple fare that was laid out on the table. There was a large bowl containing what appeared to be some type of stew and a large platter of fresh bread. She hadn't realized how hungry she was until she began eating. She discovered that it was in fact stew and was very delicious.

"Catherine told us that when you came to, you had no memory of how you got here. Is that correct?" Adam asked.

Andrea nodded her head. "I do remember leaving my home and that when it started to rain, I began to run back and that's when I must have fallen and hit my head."

Sara noticed her strained voice and interceded on her behalf. "What Andrea probably needs is a good night's sleep. Maybe in the morning she'll remember more."

Adam looked at Andrea sharply, and then glanced at his daughter. Sara obviously had taken a liking to this woman. "I agree with Sara," he said. "You're welcome to stay as long as you need to and I'll help you in any way I can."

"Thank you," Andrea said quietly.

Silence prevailed over the rest of the meal and afterward, Adam took the woman named Carol home. Andrea and the children helped Mrs. Floyd clear the table, then Sara and Daniel were sent upstairs to get ready for bed. Andrea quietly excused herself and went into the room she had first been brought to.

Gazing around the room, she realized it was a library and not the parlor as she had first assumed, for dozens of books lined the walls. She thumbed through some of them, but the names and titles were foreign to her. Looking further, she found a row of books dating back to the eighteen hundreds and a touch of excitement filled her. Maybe there would be something in one of them that might give her some information.

However, after an hour of going through most of the books, Andrea was disappointed. Sighing, she leaned back against the sofa as tears stung her eyes.

Was her father searching for her at this very moment? Did he think she had run away? What would happen to him if she never returned? Would he spend the rest of his days in debtor's prison? If so, would Saralyn be able to help him? Wearily she closed her eyes and within moments, was asleep.

Adam froze in the doorway of the library when he returned from taking Carol home and found Andrea asleep on the sofa. There was no doubt she was a beautiful woman. He had noticed that the moment she walked into the dining room. Her hair was the color of burnished gold and her skin was a light tan, as if she had been in the sun often. And her eyes were the most startling color he had ever seen. They were a light brown with flecks of green in them.

He walked over and bent down to pick up the book that was lying across her lap, and then frowning at the title, glanced at the other books on the floor. What was she doing with books about the eighteen hundreds? He wondered.

Andrea opened her eyes and found herself held with a pair of deep blue ones. When she realized who was standing over her, she pulled her gaze away and straightened up. "I'm sorry. I must have fallen asleep."

"That's understandable," Adam said, smiling. "After the ordeal you've been through, I'm surprised you're still up." He picked up the books and started putting them back on the shelves. "Interested in history?" he asked.

"You could say that," she mumbled.

"Pardon?"

"I was just passing time so that I could thank you for your hospitality," she replied.

"I told you you're welcome to stay as long as you need to."

"Mr. Rivers…"

"Please, call me Adam," he suggested.

"All right Adam," she said. "What if I never regain my memory? What will happen then?"

"We'll cross that bridge when we come to it."

"What bridge?" Andrea asked, frowning.

Adam chuckled. "It's just an expression," he explained. "Maybe you should go up and get some sleep," he suggested.

Andrea hesitated. Should she tell him the truth? Would he believe her? No, he wouldn't, she decided. "Very well," she said. "Good night."

"Good night, Andrea." He watched her leave then went over to the bar and poured himself a drink. He took a swallow and walked over to the window. The sky was covered with stars, completely opposite from the night before.

His thoughts went back to his conversation with Carol as he drove her home. She didn't believe Andrea's story about her memory loss. The cut on her head was proof that she had fallen of course, but not to remember where she came from? Carol tried to convince him that Andrea was one of those women who preyed on lonely men and took them for a ride.

He laughed to himself at being taken for a lonely man. No one had ever put him in that category.

Carol also thought Andrea should not be staying in his house, and that he should put her up in a motel. He had told her he couldn't do that. Besides, he would most likely find her family tomorrow and she would be gone.

Shaking his head, he finished his drink and turning out the light, went upstairs to bed.

***

Sara lay in her bed, staring at the ceiling, her thoughts more confused than ever. Everything Andrea told her scared her. Could it really be possible? Could she really be from the past?

She had read books on time travel and knew there were experiments on it. They even had movies about time travel. But, could it happen in real life? She wondered.

The terror she had seen in Andrea's eyes when she had brought her to the house had been real and her reaction to the bathroom and appliances in the kitchen had also been real. So if Andrea was from the past, what were they going to do? Should she tell her father? Would he believe their story?

What frightened Sara the most was the possible connection with Andrea's appearance to her and Karen playing with the Ouija board. It had kept spelling out words that hadn't made sense at the time, but did now. The one word that frightened Sara was the word 'danger'. Did it mean Andrea was in danger or was she and her family in danger? And if that were true, would there be anything she could do to stop the danger from happening?

She sighed heavily as she reached over and turned out the light.

Chapter 4

*A*ndrea awakened with the sun and stared around her for a few seconds before coming to full alertness. It wasn't a dream. She really *did* travel to the future. Her body was still sore, yet much better. Then events of the previous day came back, bringing with it sadness. She had no idea what she was going to do or how she was going to survive in this era.

She pulled back the covers and sat on the edge of the bed. The first thing she would try is that thing Sara had called a shower. She had explained that hot and cold water came from a spout in the wall and that it ran down your body.

Going into the bathroom, she opened the glass doors to the small boxed area and turned the knob with the 'H' imprinted on it, assuming that the letter meant hot. Within seconds, the water coming from the spout began to turn hot. She then turned the knob with the 'C' imprinted on it, assuming that the letter meant cold, and the water turned warm.

Removing her gown, she gingerly stepped inside the box. Surprise mixed with pleasure filled her as the water cascaded over her body. She had never experienced anything quite like this and felt she could get used to this.

She found a bar of soap and lathered her hair and body. She closed her eyes and enjoyed the tingling sensations the water was doing to her body. After several minutes, she turned the knobs and stepped out of the box, wrapping a large towel around her.

Returning to the bedchamber, she put on the clothes she had worn the night before and grimaced, wishing she had her own clothing to put on. After she had finished dressing and finally finding something to pull her hair back with, she went downstairs.

When she came downstairs, she found the children in another room across from the one she had been in last night, sitting in front of a box with bright objects moving on it. "What is that?" she whispered.

"Television," Sara replied.

"What is a television?"

"You don't know what a television is?" Daniel asked, frowning.

"It's like a bunch of pictures taken with a camera put together and is sent one frame by one frame out to the air, and signals in this box picks them up and shows it to us as completed pictures," Sara responded.

Andrea stared at her. "How do you know all this?"

Sara grinned. "I read a lot."

Andrea sat down and stared at the box. "What are you watching?" she asked.

"Cartoons," Daniel replied.

She stared at the picture for several moments, and then frowned. "Why does the coyote never capture the strange bird?"

Sara giggled, "Because if the coyote captured the road runner, the story would be over."

"He seems to get hurt a lot, but always comes back."

"It's supposed to be funny," Daniel retorted.

"I see," although she didn't. "I think I will go have a cup of coffee," she said, excusing herself.

As she was about to make her way to the kitchen, she heard someone call her name. Turning around, she saw Adam Rivers standing in the open doorway of the room she had been in last night.

"How are you feeling this morning?" he asked her as she walked toward him.

"Better, thank you," she replied.

"Have you been able to remember anything more?" he asked, motioning for her to come into the room.

"I'm afraid not," she replied, sitting down on the sofa.

"Do you mind if I ask you some questions?" he inquired quietly.

"What sort of questions?" Andrea returned, stiffening slightly.

"Simple ones that might help jog your memory," Andrea nodded and he continued. "Catherine said you were wearing a gown that looked like it dated back in the 1800's and thought that you might have been at a masquerade party. Is that possible?"

"I don't think so," she replied, shaking her head. "No, I'm sure I wasn't at any party."

"Then why you were dressed as you were?"

She wanted to tell him that she always dressed that way for dinner, but decided against it. "I really do not know," she replied.

"Could someone be looking for you? Parents, a husband?"

Pain filled her as she thought of her father. "No," she whispered. "There's no one."

"Daniel said you thought this was your house. Why would you think that?"

"I was just confused, that's all," she replied. She stiffened when she saw the look of doubt in his eyes. "Mr. Rivers, I do not know why I said those things, except as I said, I was confused. If you would like for me to leave, then I will retrieve my gown and do so."

"I never said I wanted you to leave," he told her quietly.

"Then why are you pressuring me with all these questions?"

"I wasn't aware that I was pressuring you," he stated coolly. "I was merely asking questions that might help."

"I'm sorry," Andrea whispered, rubbing her temples with her fingertips. "I know you are trying to help, but I truly do not remember anything more."

"I apologize if I have upset you, Ms. Marsh," he said quietly. "Why don't you go have Catherine make you some breakfast and we'll talk later."

"Thank you," she whispered.

Adam watched her leave with a frown on his face. What was she hiding? He wondered silently. Should he call the police and report her as a missing person? Was there someone out there looking for her right now? He sighed heavily as he grabbed his jacket and headed for the front door.

Andrea found no one in the kitchen so she poured herself a cup of coffee from some kind of machine that was on the counter and sat down at the table. She took a sip of the hot brew and grimaced at the taste. It wasn't as strong as she liked, but it was coffee.

She sighed as she thought about what she was going to do while she was here. She had no idea how long she would be here or how she would survive. She knew she couldn't stay here indefinitely, but the only skills she had were raising horses and keeping books. Maybe Mr. Rivers could help her find work somewhere.

"Good morning," Mrs. Floyd said, interrupting her thoughts as she came into the kitchen.

"Good morning," Andrea replied, smiling.

"Would you like some breakfast?" Mrs. Floyd asked. "Everyone else has already eaten, but I would be glad to fix you something."

"That won't be necessary," Andrea told her. "Coffee is fine right now."

"Well, I have some cleaning to do, so why don't you take a walk and see if you can find the stables. Mr. Rivers has some mighty fine thoroughbreds that might interest you."

"Would you like me to help you do your chores?" Andrea asked.

"No, no, I can handle the cleaning," she replied. "You go out and enjoy this beautiful day."

"Mrs. Floyd, I hope I'm not out of line by asking this, but where is Mrs. Rivers?"

A sad expression crossed Mrs. Floyd's face. "Mrs. Rivers passed away over a year ago."

"I'm so sorry. I had no idea."

"It's taken some time for the wounds to heal, but I think this family is finally getting back on track."

"I'm sure," Andrea said quietly.

"Well, I have to get to my work," Mrs. Floyd said.

Andrea smiled as Mrs. Floyd left. She poured herself another cup of coffee and sat back down at the table. There was a newspaper lying at the other end and she reached over and picked it up.

She shook her head in amazement at the pictures she saw and the stories she read; people dying from gunshot wounds, being critically injured in automobile accidents. She gazed at the picture of the machine all crumpled and shuddered. If so many people were being hurt in those things, why use them? Was that the only transportation in this era? Shaking her head, she laid the paper back down and placing her empty cup in the sink, went out the back door.

She wondered if the stables were located in the same place in this time as in her time, and took the stone path that led around the side of the house. Within minutes, she was standing in front of the stables.

They were indeed in the same place; however, these stables were much larger than the ones in her time.

Opening the door, she went inside and squealed with delight at all the beautiful horses she saw.

She walked over to a stall where an Appaloosa was staring at her. She gently rubbed his nose and began speaking to him in a whisper.

That's where Adam found her shortly before noon. He watched in absolute awe as she talked to Max. He was quite amazed to see Max nuzzling her hand for more of the food she held there. Max was one of the horses he was planning to take to auction next week because he had been unable to train him.

"You're unbelievable," he told her as he walked over to where she stood with Max. "I've had three different trainers working with Max and no one has been able to get even this close to him."

"Max," Andrea whispered to the horse. "That's a beautiful name."

"How did you do it?" Adam asked.

"It just takes patience," she replied.

"Well, you're truly amazing," he told her. "Max was due to go to auction next week."

"Why would you want to get rid of him?" she asked, surprised.

"I paid a great deal of money for him and haven't had any success in training him."

Andrea patted Max's snout and began leading him back to his stall. "Did anyone think he might have a reason for not responding?" she asked.

"What reason could there be, other than stubbornness?" he returned.

"Max is deaf, Mr. Rivers," she said quietly, turning to face him.

"Deaf?" he repeated, stunned. "How do you know that?"

"I've been around horses all my life, Mr. Rivers, and know when something is wrong with one of them."

He noted that she kept calling him Mr. Rivers, but let it pass for now. "You must be beginning to remember more about yourself," he said quietly.

Andrea stiffened slightly, shaking her head. "When I walked in here, it felt familiar, like I was at home." She turned back around and waved a hand around. "You have a lot of beautiful horses here and most of them are worth a lot of money."

"You're right," he agreed. He ran a hand thoughtfully across his chin. "How would you like work with Max and a couple of the other horses?" he asked. "Only until we can locate your family, of course." he added noting the frown crease her brow.

"You would let me do that?" she asked, surprised.

He laughed softly. "You seem to have a way with them and if you can handle Max, you can handle any horse."

"Only until I can go home," she said, excitement building inside her.

"Until you can go home," he agreed, smiling. "Now, how about some lunch? I'm starving."

"Lunch sounds great," she agreed. "Let me clean up and I'll be right there."

She was so excited; she could barely contain her laughter. As soon as Adam was out the door, she let out a squeal. She couldn't believe what just happened. Adam had offered her a job, one that she would truly love. She kissed Max on the nose and after washing her hands, headed back to the house humming a soft tune as she went.

***

During lunch, Adam announced that Andrea would be working with Max to help get him broke in while she was here. Daniel reacted with scorn, saying that a woman shouldn't be allowed to work with horses. Sara made no comment as she watched the excitement in Andrea's eyes.

After lunch was finished, Andrea returned to the stable while the children went down to the lake. She spent the rest of the afternoon in the fenced area outside the stable, working with Max and enjoying every minute of it.

After several hours, she put him back in his stall and went upstairs to clean up before dinner.

When she entered the bedchamber, she noticed something lying on the bed. Curious, she went over and picked it up and discovered it was a dress. It was a simple dress made of soft white cotton with the sleeves tapered at the wrist. She smiled when she noticed it buttoned down the front and not the back. She briefly wondered who the dress belonged to and who had left it for her.

Glancing at the timepiece on the table beside the bed, she was glad to see she had time to take another shower in the box before dinner.

Again, the water coming from the wall amazed her as she scrubbed the dirt and smell of Max from her body.

After her shower, she put on the dress and began removing the tangles from her hair. She frowned at the curls that started to form alongside her face. She decided to let the tresses fall in their usual arrangement instead of pulling them back.

Picking up the clothes she had worn that day, she grimaced at the odor. She supposed she would have to take them down to the lake and wash them. Tossing them in a corner of the room, she glanced at her reflection one last time and silently thanked whoever had left her the dress. It was a little snug across the breast and came just above her ankles, but otherwise fit her perfectly. She actually felt pretty for the first time since her arrival in this era.

She was unprepared for the reaction she received from Adam when she entered the parlor a few minutes later. His eyes registered first shock, and then a look she had never before seen entered his eyes. From the smile on Sara's face, Andrea knew she had been the one who left the dress for her.

"Good evening," she said quietly. "I hope I'm not late."

"No, of course not," Adam responded, clearing his throat. "Would you like something to drink before dinner?" he asked, moving to the bar. His hands shook as he refilled his glass. Andrea was more beautiful than she had been this morning. How was that possible?

"No, thank you," Andrea replied, smiling.

"Doesn't she look pretty, Dad?" Sara asked, walking over to where Andrea stood and taking one of her hands in both of hers. Andrea gave her a sharp look but Sara only smiled in return.

Before Adam could respond, Carol spoke from the sofa. "I would like another one, Adam." She got up and walked over and handed him her glass. Adam filled it with a generous portion of bourbon and handed it back to her.

She smiled sweetly at him and turned to face Andrea. "No one has been able to locate your family, Ms. Marsh. Why do you suppose that is?" she asked, smiling coldly at Andrea.

Andrea stiffened. Who was this woman and why was she always here? She wondered. Was she to be the next Mrs. Rivers?

"Savannah is a very large town, Ms. Masters. I'm sure it will take some time to locate my family," Andrea responded.

"But surely someone around here would know who you are," Carol argued.

Before Andrea could respond, Mrs. Floyd entered and announced that dinner was ready. Andrea released a soft sigh as she followed Sara from the room. She couldn't help but notice that Carol moved next to Adam and took his arm possessively.

During dinner, the children monopolized the conversation, which was a relief to Andrea. She didn't think she could survive another round of questions.

Carol silently watched Andrea as she listened to the children's chatter. She had tried talking to Adam again, but to no avail. He refused to listen to anything she had to say on the subject. He seemed to believe this woman's story of not remembering anything; and the nerve of him offering her a job! What was he thinking?

She glanced over at Adam who seemed to be listening to the children. Was he attracted to this woman? Was that why he refused to listen to her?

Well, she thought, if he wouldn't pursue her story, she would.

After the meal was completed, Andrea excused herself, saying she was tired. She had just finished changing clothes when she heard a soft knock at the door. A moment later, Sara entered.

"Are you really tired or did you just say that to get away from Carol?" Sara asked.

Andrea frowned. "Why would I do that?" she returned.

Sara shrugged her shoulders. "I saw the looks she was giving you at dinner. I just assumed you wanted to get away from her as quickly as possible."

Andrea chuckled softly. "She was giving me some awful looks, wasn't she?" Sara nodded, smiling. "I suppose Ms. Masters doesn't like me very much."

"She's just jealous," Sara said. "After all, you are a lot prettier than she is."

Color stained Andrea's cheeks as she shook her head. "Mrs. Floyd told me about your Mother. I'm truly sorry," she said quietly.

Sara nodded her head. "She died a little over a year ago and I know dad has to get on with his life, but why Carol?"

Your father seems quite taken with her."

Sara grunted. "The only thing my father is taken with is the sex he gets from her."

"Sara!" Andrea gasped. "Surely you don't mean that!"

"What? That I know they have sex? I'm not stupid. I know what goes on between a man and woman when they're attracted to each other."

"Does your father pay for her services?" Andrea whispered.

She spoke so softly, Sara wasn't sure she heard her. "Pay for her ser…"her eyes rounded as she let out a giggle. "No, he doesn't pay for her services," she replied.

"Then, I don't understand," Andrea said, confused.

Sara sighed as she looked at Andrea. She really didn't understand. The disbelief on her face was genuine. The fact that she had been telling the truth finally hit her and tears stung the back of her eyes. She and Karen had done this to Andrea.

"In our time, sex is an every day topic of conversation. Men and women live together without benefit of marriage and parents discuss sex with their children at length," she said softly.

Shock registered on Andrea's face as Sara's words sunk in. "You believe me!" she whispered.

"Yes," Sara whispered back, wiping at a tear that had escaped.

"Thank you!" Andrea cried, taking both of Sara's hands into hers. "So, what do we do now?"

"I have no idea," Sara responded, sighing. "No idea whatsoever."

Chapter 5

"*I* don't think it would be a good idea to tell anyone else," Sara suggested as she sat beside Andrea on the bed. "No one would believe such a story."

"But you do," Andrea said.

"That's because I finally accept responsibility for you being here," Sara replied.

"Why do you think you are responsible?" Andrea asked.

Sara told her everything that had transpired the night of the storm. How she and her friend had used the Ouija board, the words it spelled out, how the board had flown across the room. Andrea had interrupted her at that point and asked what a Ouija board was.

"It's a board game that you ask questions and it spells out answers. Some people believe that it is powerful and has connections to the other side and that you can actually talk to friends and loved ones who have passed on."

"It sounds like something evil," Andrea murmured.

Sara nodded her head. "Some people believe it is black magic and use it to conjure up the devil. But lots of people believe it is just a game board and use it for fun."

"If this is just a game, then why would you blame yourself for my being here?"

"Because Karen and I were trying to talk to my Mother through the board and it started spelling out words like danger and death. It scared both of us really bad and then the next morning, Daniel and I found you dressed in that gown and acting weird. I really thought you were crazy until you showed me those pictures," Sara finished as the tears ran freely down her cheeks.

"This Ouija board does sounds like voodoo or black magic and I do not believe in either," Andrea told her. "So, it is not your fault that I am here," she assured Sara. "Do you want to know what I believe?" she asked quietly. Sara nodded and Andrea continued. "I believe that when I fell and hit my head, I died."

"Why do you believe that?"

"The night my mother died, I was very frightened, and she told me not to be afraid of death, that dying was like falling asleep in one world and waking up in another."

"If you died in your world, then where is your body?" Sara asked, confused. "Is it just lying there on the ground or has it disappeared as well?"

A shudder passed through Andrea. "I don't know," she whispered. "But I fear that if my body is not found, my father could be in serious trouble."

"Would he be blamed for your disappearance?"

"Not by the authorities, but one man in particular," Andrea replied. "I told you my father and I had argued and I ran from the house. But I didn't tell you why we argued."

"What happened?"

"After my mother died, my father became very despondent. He began drinking and gambling. I suppose he was lonely and didn't know exactly what to do with himself."

"One night he was playing cards at one of the gaming houses and sure that he could win, made a wager with the gentleman he was playing with. Unfortunately for me, he lost the wager."

"What was the wager?" Sara whispered, caught up in Andrea's story.

"Since my father had no more money to bet, the gentleman told my father that if he won, he would walk away with clear title to our plantation and the one next to ours. But if he lost the wager, this gentleman would have my hand in marriage."

"You're kidding?!" Sara gasped.

"No, I'm not," Andrea replied, shaking her head.

"I take it your father lost and you refused to marry this man," Sara surmised.

"I despised the man and my father knew it," Andrea said angrily.

"But he must have loved you very much to force your father into such an agreement," Sara said.

"The man knows nothing of love," Andrea spat. "He only wanted me because he couldn't have me."

"He sounds like a real pig," Sara said in disgust.

"You remember the paintings we found in the attic?" Andrea asked.

"Yes," Sara replied slowly.

"Sara, your great, great grandfather, Nathan Rivers, was the man my father made the wager with."

"No way!" Sara gasped.

"Yes," Andrea said.

Sara frowned as she thought of something. "We know you didn't marry Nathan, because you're here."

"Right," Andrea agreed.

"Then how did we end up with this house?"

Andrea looked at her in puzzlement. "What do you mean?"

"When Daniel and I found you, you kept insisting that you lived here. If that's true and you believed this was your house, how did Nathan Rivers gain control of it?"

A pained expression crossed Andrea's features. "Nathan must have foreclosed on my father," she said softly.

"Then, what happened to your father?"

"I don't know," Andrea whispered, tears shining in her eyes.

"Well, we're gonna find out," Sara said, taking Andrea's hand. "Some how, some way, we'll find out what happened to your father."

"Thank you, Sara," she whispered. "Thank you for believing me and wanting to help me."

"You're welcome," Sara responded.

"There was one other thing I wanted to ask you."

"What is that?"

"Can you tell me what that thing is that chimes throughout the house? Andrea asked. "I heard it last night and again this morning."

Sara frowned, trying to think of what she could be talking about. "You mean the telephone?" she finally returned.

"I guess so, it chimes a couple of times, then stops."

"A telephone is something you use when you want to talk to someone. Like, when I want to talk to Karen, I use the telephone."

"Is it the same thing as the telegraph?"

"Sort of," Sara replied. "Only instead of sending a telegraph to someone and having to wait for a response, you can use the telephone and talk to them right then."

"It is all so confusing, trying to learn everything in your world," Andrea whispered.

"You'll get used to everything in time," Sara assured her. "Now, why don't you get some sleep and I'll see you tomorrow," she suggested.

"Very well," she agreed.

Sara closed the door softly behind her and Andrea crawled in between the sheets. She looked around the room as tears fell silently down her cheeks. "Daddy, where are you?" she whispered in a tiny voice.

For a long time Andrea lay awake, wondering what had happened to her father and afraid of the consequences if her body was never found in her world.

***

Adam poured himself another cup of coffee and sat down at the kitchen table. He was glad Carol had driven herself over here tonight because he didn't think he could have listened to her complaining about Andrea again if he'd taken her home. He needed to think. He started by adding together everything he had so far.

First, he'd found her in the library with several history books scattered all over the floor. It was as if she were trying to find something.

Second, there was Andrea's conversation with Sara and Daniel he had overheard about the television and the cartoons they were watching. She seemed genuinely confused when Sara tried to explain what a television was and what cartoons were.

Third, was her apparent fear of his questions about her memory loss and why he wasn't able to find anyone in Savannah who knew her or the name Marsh.

And last but not least, was the gown she had been wearing when Sara and Daniel found her. Catherine said that it was a gown that looked like it had been made from the nineteenth Century, and one that someone would wear to a masquerade party. But Andrea had said that she didn't remember being at any party.

He finished his coffee and got up and poured another one. Hell, if he didn't know better, he would swear she *was* from the nineteenth Century.

The cup froze halfway to his lips at what he just thought sunk in. Was it possible? Could she actually be from another century? Could she somehow have traveled through time? He knew there were theories on time travel, experiments and all that, but could it actually happen?

"Don't be stupid!" he berated himself out loud. "There's no way this woman could have traveled through time and space."

If not time travel, then how did she get here? Where did she come from? And most importantly, what was he going to do about her?

He put the cup still full of coffee in the sink and turning out the kitchen light, headed upstairs.

***

"She's dead," Jonathan said quietly.

"She's not dead!" Nathan snapped, pacing back and forth in front of the hearth.

"Then, where is she?"

Nathan stopped his pacing and turned to stare at him. "I'm beginning to think Andrea ran away just to keep from marrying me," he said.

Jonathan shook his head. "It's true she didn't want to marry you," he said. "But, she wouldn't have ran away to keep from doing it. She knew what would have happened if she refused your offer."

"Where's Saralyn?" Nathan asked, suddenly remembering that he hadn't seen her all day.

"She got a message that her mother was ill, so she had to return to Atlanta," Jonathan replied.

"That seems kind of sudden," he said, narrowing his eyes. "Did you happen to see this message?"

"Yes, I did," Jonathan responded coldly, knowing what Nathan was insinuating. "Andrea would never put Saralyn in a position where she would have to lie to me."

Nathan snorted and resumed his pacing, becoming angrier by the minute. What was so bad about marrying him? He was a very wealthy man and not bad to look at. He had women from every town he had been in chasing after him. So why was Andrea so disgusted with the thought of marriage to him? He would have given her everything she asked for.

"My little girl is gone," Jonathan whispered.

"You're drunk, old man," Nathan said disgustingly. "Go on up to bed and get out of my sight."

"I'm not drunk. I've only had two drinks," Jonathan replied stonily. "What's going to happen now, Nathan?" Jonathan asked. "What am I going to do without my little girl?"

"We'll find her. That I promise you," Nathan stated coldly.

Jonathan stood up and staggered to the door. "She's a good girl. She wouldn't run away," he mumbled.

Nathan watched him leave then walked over and poured himself a drink. Andrea had definitely disappeared. He had called the authorities and a search of the entire area had been done, with no trace of her, except the one shoe that Jonathan had found. No one on the neighboring plantations had seen her. He even had the authorities search the train station and the other counties, but nothing. It was like she had just vanished from the face of the earth.

He downed his drink and poured another. Now what was he going to do about Jonathan? The man was clearly upset about his daughter's disappearance and if he were honest with himself, he would see that Jonathan had nothing to do with it. Would he now have the authorities arrest him and foreclose on Briarcliff? Could he actually be that cruel?

Some people thought he was, but he wasn't. Just because he was a hard man to deal with in business and got what he went after, people assumed he was a bad person.

He sighed as he sat down and stared into the fire. He really had wanted Andrea for his wife. From the very first time he had seen her, he knew she would be his. Her haughty attitude had only intrigued him. Her refusal to have anything to do with him only fueled his desire for her even more.

Again, he wondered what he was going to do. Truth be known, he could never throw Jonathan in debtor's prison or have him evicted from his home. He just didn't know what to do at this moment.

He finished his drink and sure that tomorrow would bring better news, left.

Chapter 6

Andrea woke before dawn and dressed in another pair of trousers and flannel shirt that Sara had given her the day before. She crept down the stairs, careful not to awaken anyone and went quietly through the kitchen and out the back door. She followed the same stone path to the stables that she had taken the day before.

Max whinnied when she spoke to him and patted his nose. She opened the stall door and went inside and began rubbing him down all the while talking softly to him.

Mrs. Floyd was the only one in the kitchen when Adam went downstairs that morning. "Where is everyone?" he asked her.

"The children haven't come down yet," she replied.

"What about Ms. Marsh?"

"I haven't seen her this morning." She eyed him thoughtfully. "You look like you didn't get much sleep last night," she remarked.

"I didn't," Adam admitted.

Just as she was pouring Adam a cup of coffee, Daniel burst through the door. "Whoa!" Adam said, grabbing his arm.

"I'm hungry!" Daniel cried, pulling out of Adam's grasp.

"You're always hungry," Sara stated walking in after Daniel. "Where's Andrea?" she asked.

"She hasn't come down yet," Adam replied.

"She's not in her room," Sara said.

"She's probably already out at the stables," Mrs. Floyd said.

"Did she eat before she went?" Adam asked.

"Don't think so," Mrs. Floyd replied.

"That's dumb," Daniel interjected. "Who would want to skip breakfast?"

"Not you, that's for sure," Adam laughed, ruffling the top of his head.

"You two sit down," Mrs. Floyd told them. "Breakfast is ready."

"Andrea was really excited about working with Max," Sara said as she sat down across from her father.

"She said she'd been around horses all her life," Adam said.

"She told you that?" Sara asked, frowning.

"Yes, she did," Adam replied. "From the way she was handling Max, it was apparent that she knew what she was doing."

Sara released the breath she had been holding and smiled at her father. "She did say that she felt at ease around them."

"Did she tell you anything else?" he inquired.

Sara hesitated. Should she tell him the truth? How would he react if she came right out and said, "Andrea was struck by lightening in eighteen hundred eighty-nine and died. She then traveled through time and ended up here." He would probably take her straight to a psychiatrist and have Andrea arrested.

"Sara, did you hear me?" Adam said, interrupting her thoughts.

"I'm sorry. What did you say?"

"Did Andrea tell you anything else?" he repeated.

"All she told me was that she remembered she had a father and that she liked horses."

Adam had been watching Sara's face when he had asked her the question. After her answer, he felt there was something more she wanted to say, but was afraid. He wouldn't press her on it now.

He finished breakfast and pulled away from the table. "I'll be home early tonight," he told them.

"Are you going out with Carol again?" Daniel asked sullenly.

"Just to dinner," Adam responded.

"Dad?" Sara stopped him at the door. "Is it okay if Wes drives Andrea and me into town this afternoon? I thought if she saw some familiar surroundings, she might remember some more."

"All right, but be back before I leave so you can watch Daniel," he told her.

"I don't need a babysitter!" Daniel cried. "I can take care of myself."

"I'll see you two later," he said, ignoring Daniel's outburst.

After he left, Daniel went outside and Sara went to do her chores. By the time she had finished, it was close to noon so she went to the stables to talk to Andrea.

"What are you doing?" she gasped when she found Andrea cleaning the stalls.

"I'm working," Andrea replied.

"You're supposed to be working with the horses, not cleaning stalls," Sara said, grabbing the rake from her grasp.

"Cleaning the stalls is part of caring for the horses, Sara," Andrea told her. "Now, give me the rake back so I can finish."

Sara shook her head. "Lenny's supposed to clean the stalls. It's his job," she argued.

"Don't you have chores or something to do?" Andrea asked, exasperated.

"Already done," Sara replied, grinning at her. "Besides, you need to get cleaned up so we can go to town."

"What for?"

"So we can go to the public library where we can do an extensive search on my family."

"How would we get there?" When Sara didn't respond immediately, Andrea's eyes rounded in horror. "I'll not be riding in one of those machines," she declared.

"It'll be safe, I promise."

"If those machines are so safe, why do people die in them?" Andrea wanted to know.

"Accidents are caused by careless drivers and Wes is a very good driver," Sara assured her.

Andrea sighed heavily. "Is this the only place we can do this search?"

"It's the only place I know that has a genealogy section, other than the Internet, where we can trace anybody's ancestors." Andrea still hesitated, so Sara told her that Wes would drive real slow so she wouldn't be frightened.

"What is an Internet?"

"It's where people go on the computer to access information all around the world."

Andrea frowned. "What is a computer?"

"It's sort of like a typewriter, only better. A computer has lots of programs you can use for bookkeeping, writing letters, that sort of thing and the Internet is where you can get information you want or need." At Andrea's continued frown, she sighed. "I really don't know that much about computers right now, but am taking a class in school so I can learn more. I think it's better if we just go to the library to get the information we need."

"All right," Andrea agreed. "But, if I don't like riding in your automobile, I am walking," she threatened.

"It'll be okay," Sara said, smiling. "Now, go get cleaned up and we'll go after lunch." She placed the rake against the wall and went in search of Wes.

After Andrea had showered and they had eaten lunch, she climbed into the backseat of the automobile with Sara. She gritted her teeth and held tightly to the armrest on the door as Wes slowly pulled out of the drive.

She began to relax as she spotted the many tall buildings that came into view. "I have never seen anything like this. It… it's unbelievable."

Sara managed a smile. "Yes," she agreed, looking around at the buildings.

"In my time, the roads are dirt and cobblestone and the buildings are single stories and made mostly of wood and brick."

"There are still some streets like that in the older section of Savannah. Maybe we can ride down there one day so you can see that some things haven't changed too much."

"That would be nice," Andrea murmured.

"I imagine this is quite a shock to you."

Andrea was in total awe as they pulled up in front of a four-story building.

She followed Sara inside and stood beside her while she asked the woman behind a long table where the genealogy section was located.

Andrea followed Sara staring at the thousands of books on shelves as they came to a small room with more books and funny looking machines.

She stood behind Sara as she sat down at one of the machines and started looking through a small cabinet. "What are you doing?" she finally asked.

"I'm looking for microfilm with dates in the 1800's," Sara replied.

"What is a microfilm?"

"Microfilm is condensed versions of newspapers and articles that you look at through this machine," Sara replied, pointing to the machine on the table.

Andrea shook her head. "Your world is very confusing," she whispered.

Sara smiled. "You'll get used to it."

"I don't think so," Andrea mumbled.

After two hours of going through old newspaper clippings and articles, the only thing Sara found was a story about Nathan Rivers running for the Senate in the early 1900's. It didn't give a lot of detail about Nathan, only that he was the President and CEO of the Bank of Savannah and had resided in Savannah for several years. That he was married and had two children. The names of his wife and children were not listed.

Disappointed and darkness beginning to fall, they left the library and climbed back into the car.

Andrea was quiet on the way back and Sara tried to tell her not to give up, that their search was far from over. Andrea only nodded her response as she watched the scenery outside the car window.

When they arrived home, Andrea went up to her room and Sara did not follow her, sensing that she needed time alone.

***

At the same time Sara and Andrea were at the library going through microfilm and old newspaper clippings, Adam was in his office on the 7th floor of the Park Manor building in downtown Savannah. He was searching the Internet for any families named Marsh located in Savannah and the surrounding areas.

Unfortunately, he wasn't having any luck. The only Marshes he found were dead, leaving no descendants, and two young women, who had no relative by the name of Andrea, living or dead.

He then extended his search for the entire state of Georgia, but still had no luck. No one by the name of Andrea Marsh lived in this state. Frustrated, he disconnected with the Internet. He could question her again, insisting that she tell him the truth. But what if she were telling the truth, that she had no memory of what happened to her?

On the other hand, what if there was some merit to his theory? What if she really did travel through time?

He was jerked out of his thoughts by the telephone on his desk ringing. His thoughts about Andrea were momentarily forgotten when his secretary informed him that the CEO of Barker & Barker Investments was on the telephone.

***

After her father and Mrs. Floyd had left for the evening, Andrea still had not come downstairs, so Sara and Daniel ate dinner alone.

"Do you think Dad is going to marry Carol?" Daniel asked Sara after several moments of silence.

"I don't know, Danny," Sara replied.

"I hope not," he mumbled. "Do you like her?"

Sara shook her head. "Not really."

"Me neither," Daniel agreed. "Why doesn't she like us?" he asked.

"I think it's just that she's not used to kids, that's all."

"Uh-uh," he said, shaking his head. "She acts like she really hates us."

Sara frowned. "Dad wouldn't marry someone that hates his kids," she told him.

"What about Andrea? You like her, don't ya?"

"Yea, I do," she replied, smiling.

"I think she's weird."

"She's not weird, just different."

"I don't think she likes me cause of how I treated her when she first came here," he said sullenly.

"Well, I think if you apologize and be nice to her, you'll find out that she really does like you."

"Okay," he agreed grudgingly. "But if she doesn't like me then, I'm not gonna like you anymore."

Sara laughed as she playfully slapped him on the arm.

When Andrea did finally come down stairs later that night, she found Sara and Daniel in the kitchen. She inquired as to what they were doing, and laughing, Sara told her they were making popcorn.

Sara nudged Daniel, indicating that now was the time for him to apologize to Andrea.

Shuffling his feet, Daniel looked up at Andrea and smiled shyly. "I'm sorry I treated you so mean when you first came."

Her eyes widened in surprise as she glanced over at Sara. Sara smiled and nodded her head.

Andrea looked down at Daniel. "I accept your apology," she told him quietly.

Daniel looked at Sara and grinned.

"Now, will you tell me about this popcorn?" Andrea asked.

That night, Andrea was introduced to her first taste of popcorn and her first motion picture on a television.

***

"Aren't you coming in?" Carol asked when Adam didn't turn the car engine off.

"It's been a long day and I'm really tired," he replied.

"Just for a few minutes, please?" she asked.

Adam sighed as he turned the engine off, got out of the car, and followed Carol up to her apartment.

"Would you like a drink?" she asked, walking over to the bar.

"I'll have a quick one, and then I need to get home," Adam replied.

Carol poured two glasses of bourbon and handed one to Adam. She sat down on the sofa and patted the cushion next to her. Adam hesitated a moment, then sat down.

Carol sipped her drink as she watched Adam beneath lowered lashes. He was the most delicious man she had ever met and wanted him more than ever at this very moment. She reached over and gently laid her hand on his thigh.

Adam downed his drink and stood. "I really should get home," he said. "I promised the kids I wouldn't be out too late."

Carol gritted her teeth. "Do you really have to go?"

"Yea," he replied. "Thanks for the drink. I'll see you later."

Carol frowned slightly. "You haven't forgotten that you're taking me to the Ramsey dinner party tomorrow night, have you?"

"No, I haven't forgotten," he replied. Actually, he had.

"Then, I'll see you at seven," she said, smiling.

"At seven," he agreed.

The smile disappeared from her face the minute the door shut behind him. She finished her drink and grabbed the telephone. She dialed a number and it was answered on the third ring.

"Get your ass down here now," she grated into the receiver.

"Do you have any idea what time it is?" the man at the other end said.

"I don't give a damn!" Carol snapped. "I need you here now!"

"Problems with lover boy?" he sneered.

"No," she ground out. "I just need for him to be distracted for a little while. So, catch the next flight that's available and get here," she slammed down the receiver and poured herself another bourbon. She took a long swallow and swore softly as it burned her throat.

She was angry with Adam for his treatment of her tonight. He had been very quiet throughout dinner and didn't seem to hear anything she said.

She had worn one of her sexiest outfits and put on his favorite perfume, but to no avail. She had tried several times during dinner to pull him into conversation, but he kept drifting in and out.

Carol was sure he had been occupied with thoughts of Andrea and knew he was attracted to her. She had to admit Andrea was pretty, but definitely not Adam's type. It brought to mind his dead wife, Amanda. That woman had been a fool as far as she was concerned. When you had a man like Adam, why would you want any other man?

81

Well, Amanda had been taken out of the picture, leaving a clear path for her and she'd be damned if she was going to let Andrea get in her way.

She finished her drink and picked up the telephone again. After her conversation this time, she hung up smiling.

***

The sight that met Adam's eyes when he walked into the living room would forever be imprinted on his mind. Sara was asleep on the floor and Daniel was curled up on Andrea's lap with his head nestled in the valley between her breasts. He felt a pang of envy that it was his son's head and not his resting there.

He bent down and gently shook Sara awake and told her to go up to bed. He then slowly disengaged Daniel from Andrea, careful not to wake her, and carried him upstairs.

Andrea was still sleeping when he returned, so he sat down in the chair across from her and watched as her breasts rose and fell with each breath.

She had been on his mind all day and all night. He had barely contained his annoyance with Carol until the evening had come to an end.

Andrea moaned softly and he kneeled down in front of her. His heart did a flip when she opened her eyes and smiled at him.

"Did I do it again?" she asked softly.

"Do what?" he returned, clearing his throat.

"Fall asleep on your sofa," she replied, yawning.

"Afraid so," he replied, smiling. He noticed the traces of tears on her face and frowned. "Have you been crying?" he asked quietly.

Andrea touched her cheek and smiled. "We were watching a moving picture that was sad," she replied.

Adam's frown deepened; moving picture? He thought to himself; another piece to the puzzle. "You mean a video?" he asked.

"Yes, a video," she replied, wondering what she had said wrong.

He stood as she unfolded her legs from underneath her. Adam caught her as she swayed and tried to stand.

Andrea was lost in the dark pool liquid of his eyes as she gazed up at him. Her breath caught in the back of her throat as he tipped his head and lightly brushed her lips with his. She moaned softly as the kiss deepened and would have fallen had he not wrapped his arms around her. A tingling sensation began in the pit of her stomach and traveled down to the area between her legs when she felt the tip of his tongue slip between her lips.

The kiss seemed to go on forever when he finally pulled back. "You should go to bed," he whispered.

"Yes," she breathed, pulling out of his arms. "Good night, Adam."

It was several seconds before Adam could respond and when he did, the room was empty.

He cursed softly as he took off his jacket and loosened his tie. Why had he kissed her? He knew absolutely nothing about her. So why was he so attracted to her? Why did he want to go up to her room right this minute and make love to her?

Why didn't he just call the police and file a missing report as Carol had suggested? What was he afraid of? Was he afraid he would find out she was who Carol said she was and possibly never see her again? And if he did call the police and she was taken away, what would that do to Sara and Daniel? He knew Sara was very attached to her and it seemed after tonight, Daniel was also becoming attached to her. Could he put his children through another crisis?

He picked up his jacket and tie and turning out the lights, went up to bed having come to no conclusion of what he was going to do.

Chapter 7

*A*dam woke the next morning with no solution to his dilemma, but since it was the last day of the children's spring break, he decided a picnic would be the perfect way to spend the day.

When he walked into the kitchen, he found Andrea helping Catherine with breakfast. She smiled shyly at him and he found himself returning her smile.

He told them his idea about going on a picnic down by the lake and everyone agreed excitedly. Sara wanted to know if it was all right if she invited her friend, Karen. She hadn't seen Karen since that awful night and wanted to make sure she was okay. Adam told her it was all right with him, so she went to call Karen while Andrea and Mrs. Floyd prepared a basket. After breakfast, the five of them headed for the lake.

The day was filled with laughter as Daniel showed Andrea how to fish. Adam was amazed that she didn't know how to fish, but didn't question her about it. Again, it was another piece of the puzzle.

Sara and Karen were lying on a blanket a few feet away listening to the radio and watching Andrea and Daniel.

The two girls had been friends since Kindergarten. Sara had been quiet and shy and was sitting in a corner by herself. Karen had gone over and sat down beside her and had started talking to her, and from that moment on, had become good friends. Karen was a couple of months younger than Sara, but they were about the same size and their coloring was similar, except the eyes. Karen's eyes were a dark brown.

"What happened to you that night?" Sara asked Karen.

"I had to get home," Karen replied.

"You left because you were scared," Sara said.

"I was not," she saw the look on Sara's face and shrugged. "Okay, maybe a little," she admitted. "But when thunder crashed and that thing went flying across the room, it spooked me."

"It spooked me too," Sara admitted. "I haven't touched it since that night."

"How come Ms. Marsh doesn't know how to fish?" Karen asked as she watched Daniel show Andrea how to put the worm on her hook.

When Sara had introduced Karen to Andrea, she had told her that she was her mother's cousin and had come for a visit.

"I guess she's never fished before," Sara replied.

"I thought all grown-ups knew how to fish."

"Not all grown-ups," Sara said. "Maybe she never had anyone to teach her before." She rolled over on her stomach and closed her eyes.

Adam watched Andrea and Daniel together and felt a peace he hadn't felt in a long time. She seemed so natural with his children, it was as if she had been around them all their lives. Was that part of his attraction to her? He wondered.

He had no doubt if he hadn't pulled away when he did last night, he would have taken her right there on the living room floor. He knew by her response to his kiss that she wanted him as much as he wanted her. So, why hadn't he?

"Dad, she's got a big one!" Daniel cried, breaking into his thoughts.

"Well, reel him in," he said, walking over to where they stood. "Feed him a little line, then pull back hard," he instructed as he moved behind Andrea and placed his hands with hers on the pole. Within a few minutes, she had reeled in a large-mouth bass.

"Wow!" Daniel exclaimed. "That's the biggest fish ever caught out of this lake!"

Andrea felt a chill as Adam moved away from her. Color stained her cheeks when she thought about their kiss last night. She had never been kissed like that before and had wanted it to last forever. The sensations his kiss evoked in her made her curious to know more and she silently wondered if he would kiss her again.

She was brought out of her daydream by Adam telling Sara it was time to break out the picnic basket and eat lunch.

Daniel monopolized the entire conversation with talk of the fish that Andrea had caught and other times he and Adam had come fishing here while they ate sandwiches, potato salad, and pickles.

About an hour after they had eaten, Daniel and the girls began playing around in the water while Adam and Andrea sat on the blanket and watched them.

"I took Max out for a ride yesterday," Andrea said quietly.

"Any problems?" Adam asked.

She shook her head and smiled. "Didn't throw me once."

"Good," he said. "Who taught you so much about horses?" he asked.

"My parents," she responded.

"Do they still have horses?"

"My parents are dead," she whispered softly.

"Is that why you left your home?"

"I don't remember."

"Then how do you know your parents are dead?"

She shrugged. "I just know, that's all."

Sara glanced over to where Andrea and her father were sitting and noticed the expression on Andrea's face. She got out of the water and walked over to them.

"Want to come in for a swim?" she asked. Andrea breathed a sigh of relief and shook her head. "How about you, dad?"

Adam frowned at the interruption. "I think it's time we headed home," he said as he stood and called for Daniel and Karen to get out of the water.

"Thank you," Andrea mouthed to Sara.

The sun was just beginning to set as they packed up everything and headed home.

Andrea walked beside Sara and Karen, following behind Adam and Daniel. When they reached the house, she helped Sara and Karen unpack the basket and she went upstairs while Sara and Karen went to her room.

Andrea went in and took a shower and changed her clothes and when she came downstairs a short time later, she found Sara and Daniel in the living room watching television. She asked where Karen was and Sara told her that Adam had dropped her off at home on his way to a party.

Hiding her disappointment, she sat down on the sofa beside Sara and tried to concentrate on the program on television.

Andrea went to bed that night with thoughts of Adam on her mind. She hadn't asked Sara who he had gone to the party with, knowing that it had been Carol. She wondered why he hadn't told her about going out tonight. It was probably because it wasn't any of her business. But, she had thought that after their kiss and the day they'd had together at the lake, he would have at least mentioned it to her.

Maybe she was reading more into it than there was, she thought. Adam was used to being with women and probably thought their kiss was nothing more than that. It probably didn't have the same effect on him that it had on her.

Sighing softly, she closed her eyes and tried to clear the image of Adam kissing her from her mind.

***

After an hour of conversation about politics and sports, Adam had a hard time concentrating on either subject and was ready to leave the dinner party.

He could hear the women laughing where they stood across the room and glanced over at them. His eyes came in contact with Carol's and he smiled grimly as he rolled his eyes upward. She smiled back and shook her head.

"So, Adam, when are we going to get to meet this mystery woman of yours?" John Ramsey asked.

John Ramsey was a very successful attorney in Savannah and had been married to his childhood friend, Renee, for 15 years. The two of them become good friends and when their busy work schedules permitted, would often go fishing together.

Adam and Amanda had named John and Renee Godparents of their children, and since Renee was unable to have children of her own, she had become a second mother to Adam's children, especially since the death of Amanda.

"I beg your pardon?" Adam returned.

"Carol told us all about her," Sam Alford said. "It would be interesting to have a session with her."

Sam was a prominent psychiatrist in Savannah and one of the most annoying characteristics about his personality was that he tried to analyze everyone. Adam wasn't as close to Sam as John was, but still considered him one of his friends.

"Exactly what did Carol tell you?" Adam asked quietly.

"That Ms. Marsh basically showed up on your doorstep with no memory of where she came from," John answered.

"I think it's fascinating and would love to put her under hypnosis," Sam remarked. "Why don't you call my office and set up an appointment for her one day next week?" he suggested.

"Is there a possibility that she would be able to remember everything if you were to hypnotize her?" John asked Sam.

"Most cases actually are successful," Sam replied.

"How would you go about it, getting her to remember?" John asked.

"I'd take her back to the time before she had her accident, and then slowly bring her forward until most or all of her memory came back."

"Sounds like a good idea," John said. "Why don't you try that, Adam?"

"Gentlemen, if you will excuse Adam for a few minutes, I would like to talk to him about some advertising for my next show," Renee Ramsey intervened. She took Adam's arm and the two of them walked out onto the terrace.

She had been watching Adam's face as John and Sam discussed his houseguest and she could see the anger beginning to surface in the way his body was tensed.

She had been slightly intrigued by Carol's story of Andrea Marsh and how she had appeared on Adam's doorstep. However, she wasn't sure Carol was telling the whole truth about Ms. Marsh stealing another woman's identity in order to cover up some sordid past.

Adam walked over to the railing and stared up at the sky.

"I apologize for John. However, I cannot apologize for Sam," she said quietly. "I promise you John and I will have a long discussion about this at a more private time."

Adam nodded his head. "Carol had no right to discuss my personal life with anyone."

"Carol gets a little excited at times where you're concerned. She's crazy about you, you know," Renee said in Carol's defense.

"It's still none of her business," he said tightly.

"Is any of it true?" Renee asked quietly.

Adam sighed. "It's true that Sara and Daniel found Andrea in an area past the woods. She was injured and unconscious."

"Is she using another woman's identity?"

Adam hesitated momentarily. "No," he stated flatly.

"Then where did she come from, Adam? Why did she mysteriously appear on your doorstep?"

Before Adam could comment, Carol walked out on the terrace.

"Is everything all right?" she asked.

"Adam and I were just talking about my new ad campaign," Renee lied. Adam arched his eyebrow, but made no comment.

Carol walked over and took Adam's hand in hers as she smiled up at him.

"It's been a long day and I'm tired," he said. Removing his hand from Carol's grasp, he walked over to Renee and kissed her lightly on the cheek. "Thank you for a lovely dinner."

"We're leaving?" Carol asked, surprised.

"If you're not ready to go yet, I'm sure John or Sam would be more than happy to drive you home," he suggested.

Carol frowned, and shook her head. "I had a lovely evening," she told Renee. "I'll call you next week."

Renee nodded her head in assent. "I'll get with you sometime next week about that advertising campaign for my show," she told Adam.

"Fine. Tell John I'll talk to him later."

Renee nodded and went back inside. She walked over to where her husband stood with Sam and took his hand in hers.

"Adam said to tell you that he would talk to you later," she told him.

"He left?" John asked, surprised.

"You know Adam isn't big on parties, John. He was ready to leave the minute he got here."

"I don't think Adam approved of our conversation."

"Adam is a very private person and doesn't like to be the center of attention. You know that, John," she said.

John nodded agreement. "I'll be sure to call him tomorrow and make my apologies," John said.

"I'm sure you will," she said quietly, smiling. She kissed him on the cheek and returned to the group of women.

Adam was quiet as he drove Carol home. When he pulled up in front of her apartment complex, he turned the engine off and looked at her. "I would appreciate you not discussing my personal life with your friends," he said.

"They're your friends too, Adam and I didn't realize that Andrea was a secret," she told him.

"I would just prefer you not talk about her to anyone," he said.

"And why is that, Adam?"

"Because I said so," he replied tightly.

"Very well," she replied.

He got out and went around and opened the door for her, then walked back around to the driver's side.

"You aren't coming in?" she asked.

He sighed. "I'm really tired, Carol. I'll talk to you later."

She closed the car door and stood on the sidewalk and watched as he drove away.

Tears rolled down her cheeks as she let herself into her apartment. She had really been hoping he would come in and maybe stay the night with her.

She missed him and the feel of his body next to hers. Adam hadn't made love to her since Andrea had shown up.

Angrily, she wiped the tears from her face and went into her bedroom. Removing her clothes, she knew she had to get rid of Andrea Marsh before Adam lost complete interest in her.

***

Andrea rose before dawn the next morning and quietly made her way to the stables, trying not to awaken anyone. She knew the children had to attend classes today and would be waking soon, but she wasn't ready to face Adam across the breakfast table.

She was rubbing Max down when she heard someone enter the stable. Turning around, she smiled when she saw Sara.

"I was expecting to see you at breakfast this morning," she said.

"I woke early and came straight here. I wanted to get started before it became too warm," she explained.

"I'm on my way to school and wanted to tell you bye."

"Are you looking forward to getting back to your classes?" Andrea asked.

Sara shrugged. "I'd rather stay here with you."

Andrea smiled. "How long do you stay in school?"

"I get out at three and should be home by four."

"Then, I'll see you at four," Andrea told her, smiling.

"Will you be all right here by yourself?"

"I'll be fine," Andrea assured her.

"Okay. See you when I get home."

Andrea walked to the stable door and watched as Sara, Daniel and Adam drove away. She sighed heavily as she turned back to her task.

***

Adam received two telephone calls that morning. One from John, apologizing for discussing Adam's personal life in mixed company and one from Sam Alford.

Obviously, Carol had told Sam more than she had told anyone else of Andrea's appearance in his life. He begged Adam to bring Andrea in for a session. He was sure that he could help her regain her memory. Without being blatantly rude, Adam told Sam he would discuss it with Andrea and if she agreed, then he would call him to set up an appointment.

Adam was sure Andrea would never agree to such a thing, and therefore, had no intention of mentioning it to her.

That night, Andrea began slowly to develop a reason for another early retirement. Although her body and mind were attuned to Adam's every word at the dinner table, she tried to appear listless and tired.

She excused herself from the table and everyone seemed to understand as she apologized and left the room; everyone except Sara. She appeared concerned, yet puzzled. She had noticed the change in Andrea the day they had come back from the lake. Had being included in the family gathering brought back memories of her father? Was Andrea homesick and missing him and her life in the past?

Deciding that was the reason for Andrea's change in her attitude, Sara knew the best thing to do was let her work it out on her own. Andrea had every reason to be depressed, being so far away from her father and in a place where everything was strange.

The rest of the week, Andrea would have an early dinner alone in the kitchen and retire with the excuse that she was exhausted.

***

Saturday morning, Andrea was awakened by the sound of thunder rolling in the distance. She pulled back the covers and got out of bed and walked over to the window. She could see lightening far off and wondered how long before it reached here. She had a feeling of déjà vu and crossing herself, went into the bathroom.

She expected to find Sara and Daniel in front of the television and Adam gone when she came downstairs a short time later. However, to her surprise, the three of them were playing some sort of game together.

"Good morning," Adam said, smiling.

"Good morning," Andrea returned. "What are you playing?" she asked.

"Monopoly," he said. "Would you like to join us?"

"What is Mo-nop-ly?"

"You never played Monopoly?" Daniel asked.

"No, I don't believe I have," she replied, shaking her head.

"Come sit with me and I'll show you how the game is played," Sara suggested.

Andrea sat down beside Sara and concern etched her features as Daniel threw a pair of dice on the table. "Is this gambling?" she asked quietly.

"The dice are rolled to show you how many spaces you can move on the board," Sara explained as Daniel took what looked like a miniature of one of those automobile machines and began moving it around the board.

"This is gambling," Andrea said when the automobile was placed on a square and Adam handed him what appeared to be money.

Adam watched Andrea as Sara explained in detail how the game was played. He was beginning to believe the pieces of the puzzle were finally coming together. She seemed genuinely amazed at the explanation Sara gave her and he knew she was not putting on an act.

"Are we going to play or what?" Daniel piped in irritably.

"Do you want to play?" Sara asked Andrea.

"No, I'll just watch," Andrea replied, shaking her head.

Sara picked up the dice and rolled and within moments, the game was back in progress.

Andrea moved to one of the chairs near the window and watched as the three of them played and laughed throughout the game.

Sometimes, she would gaze out the window watching the rain hit the glass, her thoughts on her father and home. She couldn't help but wonder if he were still searching for her.

Every so often, Adam would glance over at Andrea and wonder what she was thinking. When she looked out the window, her expression became saddened. Was she thinking about someone she had left behind? If so, did she miss that someone?

No one realized how late it was until Daniel complained of being hungry.

"Then, why don't we get something to eat," Adam suggested.

"Can we finish the game after we eat?" Daniel inquired.

"Yes," Adam replied, laughing.

Daniel grabbed Sara's hand, pulling her from the room, leaving Adam and Andrea alone.

"Let's go see what we can find to eat," Adam said. Andrea nodded in agreement as they followed Sara and Daniel to the kitchen.

Adam found some left over fried chicken and potato salad in the refrigerator. After they had finished eating, Daniel grabbed Adam by the shirt and began pulling him toward the living room to finish their game.

"Aren't you coming?" Adam asked when Andrea didn't follow them.

"If you don't mind, I think I would like to get a book from the library and go up to my room and read for a while," she replied. Adam frowned slightly and nodded his head.

Andrea went into the library and began looking through the books on the shelves. She found one entitled, "Gone with the Wind" and taking it, went upstairs. She was surprised to learn that the book was about the war between the North and South.

So engrossed in her reading about Scarlet and her fight to save her plantation, it took several minutes to register what noise was coming from downstairs. She was sure it was music, but none she had ever heard before.

She made her way downstairs and stood in the doorway to the living room. She covered her mouth to smother a giggle as she watched Adam holding Sara's and Daniel's hands as they moved around the floor to some guy singing about stepping on his blue suede shoes.

"Andrea! Come dance with us!" Sara cried when she spotted Andrea standing in the doorway.

Andrea shook her head, but Sara grabbed her hand and pulled her forward. Placing her hand in Adam's, the four of them twirled around the room to the music.

It was several minutes before Adam and Andrea realized that Sara and Daniel had slipped quietly out of the room.

Andrea tried to pull her hand out of Adam's, but he tightened his grip and started twirling her around the room.

The music changed, became slower and Adam pulled her closer to him. He took her arms and placed them on his shoulders and wrapped his around her waist.

Andrea was finding it hard to breathe as Adam leaned in closer to her. She gasped softly as she stared into his eyes. Her heart began beating faster and heat began to surge through her body as Adam lowered his gaze to her lips and inhaled sharply. At any moment, she knew he would kiss her.

"Well, isn't this a cozy little scene." A nasty voice came from the doorway.

Andrea stiffened at the sound of Carol's voice and pulled away from Adam.

"Carol, so nice of you to drop by unannounced," Adam said dryly.

"I rang the bell, but I guess you didn't hear it with the music being so loud," she responded snidely.

"What brings you out in this weather?" Adam asked.

"If you'll excuse me, I'll leave you two alone," Andrea said quietly.

"Actually, you're the one I came to see," Carol stated, halting Andrea's flight from the room.

"Why would you want to see me?" Andrea asked quietly.

"I thought you might like to know what our investigation turned up," Carol replied.

"Not now, Carol," Adam warned in a low voice.

"Oh, come on, Adam," she said. "Surely Andrea should know that we found out she's a fraud."

"You had me investigated?" Andrea asked, turning startled eyes on Adam.

"I did—"

"Would you like to know what we found out?" Carol interrupted, ignoring the angry glint in Adam's eyes. Without waiting for a reply, she continued. "We did locate Andrea Marsh. However, she's been dead for over a hundred years."

The color drained from Andrea's face as she grabbed the corner of the sofa to steady herself.

"So, you see Ms. Whoever you are, you're nothing but a liar."

Andrea shook her head. "I am not a liar," she whispered.

"The game is over, honey, so give it up," Carol said nastily.

"That's enough!" Adam snapped, glaring at Carol.

"I'm not a liar," Andrea murmured as she turned and fled the room.

Adam turned on Carol when he heard the front door slam. "What the hell do you think you're doing?" he demanded, his voice deadly quiet.

"Come on, Adam!" she cried. "She's a fraud and now she's been exposed. The only thing left for her to do now is pack what meager belongings she has and get out."

"That's not for you to decide," he grated harshly as he headed for the front door.

"Where are you going?" Carol cried as she followed him.

"I'm going to find Andrea and when I get back, you'd better be gone," he told her coldly, slamming the door behind him.

"Damn you Adam!" she screamed at the closed door. "I'm not about to let that piece of white trash take what is mine," she vowed silently as she stormed out of the house.

Andrea felt the first drops of rain hit her as she neared the lake. She was crying so hard, she stumbled and would have fallen if not for the boulder blocking her path. She dropped to her knees and wrapped her arms around her body.

A streak of lightening split the sky and Andrea was reminded of the night she arrived in this time. Maybe if she got struck by lightening, she would be sent back to her time.

"Please, God, take me home," she whispered. "Why are you doing this to me? Why am I here?" She leaned against the boulder and let the tears fall freely.

That's how Adam found her several minutes later. "Andrea," he said softly, kneeling down beside her.

She gazed at him through her tears. "Adam?" she whispered brokenly.

"Let's go home," he said, gently lifting her into his arms.

She didn't fight him as he carried her back to the house and up to her room. He sat her down on the side of the bed and began unbuttoning her shirt. She stopped him just as he reached the last one. "I'm not a liar," she whispered brokenly.

"I know," he returned, as he unbuttoned the last button and removed her wet shirt. The imploring look in her eyes was his undoing. He took her face between his hands and gently touched her lips with his.

"I should go," he breathed, ending the kiss.

As he turned, Andrea touched his arm. "Please, don't go," she whispered.

"If I stay, you know what will happen," he warned gently.

She didn't know exactly. She only knew that she wanted to be held in his arms. "I don't want to be alone," she said softly.

His eyes searched hers, as though wanting to make sure. Slowly, with purpose, he reached up and glided his hands around the base of her head. His fingers entered her hair and he heard her quick intake of breath. Gently, he brought her face closer to his. The magnetism between them grew stronger as they neared. He felt something so intense, so compelling rushing through his body that he knew this moment was privileged, that nothing in his life had ever come close to comparing.

Her eyes never broke contact as his face barely touched hers. She could feel his breath upon her skin while they stared into the depths of each others souls.

Oh, what she saw nearly stopped the beating of her heart! It was as though she had waited her entire life for this moment.

"I want you, Andrea," He whispered the words into her mouth. "I want you so much I've got to tell you even though it may scare you and end this. I have never desired another woman as I desire you."

Her breath left her body in a rush that was almost surrender. She knew deep within her that if she proceeded, her life would never be the same.

She was astounded by the ripples of pleasure that seemed to pulse from deep within her and race along her skin. Adam moaned as if he also felt this stunning sensation. The kiss became fast and hard and when they broke away and again stared into each others eyes, they were gasping for breath.

They stood at the side of the bed, staring at each other. When he had removed her shirt, he hadn't noticed she wasn't wearing a brasserie, but a type of chemise that he had never seen before. He reached out and lightly ran his fingers down the side of her face to her neck and the laces that bound her chemise. She kept her gaze locked with his, taking her strength from him.

"I have dreamed of this moment," he whispered, pulling on the laces until the chemise was open. He gently removed it and placed it on the bed.

She drew in her breath as his hands gently touched her breasts.

Without a word, Adam removed his shirt and when his bare skin touched her breasts, she moaned with the searing contact. Her head fell back and he placed kisses along her neck and shoulder. He took his time, savoring each inch of skin. Everywhere he touched, her blood rushed to that spot, leaving her feverish.

Adam removed the remaining barrier of clothing between them. As he stood there naked, Andrea realized that she wasn't frightened. Even though she had never before seen a man naked, the sight of him standing there was the most natural thing in the world to her.

"You are so beautiful." His voice was low and husky with desire.

He picked her up and laid her gently on the bed, placing her against the soft pillows. He lowered his head and kissed her lips, her eyes, her nose, her chin. He lingered at her breasts, tasting each one as his hands roamed down her body. When his hand came in contact with the mound between her legs, she released a tiny gasp.

He kissed her tenderly as he moved to lie on top of her. Andrea gasped with the shear scorching connection as she automatically opened her legs to welcome him.

At the first penetration, she gasped. Adam lifted his head and stared at her. "Andrea?" he whispered her name in wonder.

"Don't stop," she breathed.

"Are you sure?"

"Yes," she replied, smiling shyly. She wound her arms around his neck and pulled him to her.

At the first thrust, she cried out softly. He moved slowly, and then began a rhythmic motion and Andrea followed. He brought her to the edge over and over again, urging her onward until it built and built and Andrea was flying as wave after wave of sensation coursed through her body.

"Andrea… Andrea…" he called her name as his body stiffened with release as he joined her. They clung together through the aftershocks, gasping as they crested on and on.

He lifted his head and gazed at her. "Why didn't you tell me?"

"Would you have stopped if I had?"

"I don't know," he replied honestly.

"I didn't want you to stop, Adam," she told him quietly.

He slid off her and pulled her into his arms. She lay on her side and placed her hand on his chest. He stroked her back and kissed the top of her head.

"Did I hurt you?" he queried softly.

"Only for a moment," she replied, idling running her hand through the hair on his chest. "Will it hurt again?" she asked quietly.

He chuckled softly and continued to stroke her back. "It usually doesn't hurt after the first time," he replied.

"Can we make sure?" she asked shyly.

He chuckled again as he hugged her to his chest. He lifted her chin and kissed her with such tenderness that Andrea moaned with renewed pleasure.

Her sigh filled the room as he slid over her body and stared down into her beautiful eyes.

Twice more during the night, Adam took her to places she had never imagined possible.

Chapter 8

"Andrea! Andrea! Can I come in?"

Hugging her pillow, Andrea blinked several times and saw that the space next to her was empty. Adam was gone. "Oh, Sara," she murmured sleepily. "Let me sleep for a few more minutes." She felt like she had just closed her eyes.

Sara opened the door and went in. "Why are you still in bed, and why aren't you wearing your nightgown?"

Immediately awake, Andrea pushed the hair back from her face and pulled the covers over her.

"Ah…"she stammered, fumbling for an excuse for her nakedness. "I guess I got hot in the middle of the night and removed it."

"Do you have a fever?" Sara asked, coming closer and putting her hand to Andrea's cheek.

Boy, if she only knew!

"No, I don't think so," she answered, wishing Sara would not look into her eyes so directly. Surely her night with Adam was written all over her face.

"Well, get up!" Sara told her. "Dad said we could go shopping."

Andrea straightened up. "You've seen your father this morning?"

"Yea, he's in his study, reading the newspaper."

"How did he seem?"

Sara shrugged. "A little distracted, but otherwise fine. He said it was okay for us to go to the mall today."

"What is a mall?" Andrea asked, frowning.

"It's a building full of all different kinds of shops. Probably more than you've ever seen in one place. Just wait—"

"You do not go to Mass on Sunday?" Andrea interrupted.

"We did before my mom died."

"Everyone should go to Mass," Andrea said. "It is what holds a family together."

"If you want to go, I'll go with you," Sara told her.

Andrea shook her head. "It would not be the same. I would not know anyone and I have no family to attend with me."

"We're your family now, aren't we, Andrea?"

"Probably not after what happened last night," she replied, frowning.

"What do you mean? What happened?"

Andrea relayed to her what Carol had found out from her investigation. "She called me a liar and said I was playing some kind of game with Adam."

"I don't know what my dad sees in that woman," Sara stated angrily. "She treats me and Daniel like we don't exist and walks around here like she owns the place." She looked at Andrea with concern. "Dad didn't believe her, did he?"

"He said he knew I wasn't a liar, but I think he knows I'm hiding something."

"Should we tell him?" Sara asked.

"I've thought about it, but I don't think it would be a good idea. What if he doesn't believe me and either has me arrested or tells me I have to leave. Where will I go then?"

"We have that picture of you. That's proof that you lived over a hundred years ago."

"You said yourself that it was an old picture, one you could hardly tell was me. Adam may think it's just someone who looks like me," Andrea argued.

"You're right," Sara said, sighing. "Maybe if we can find something more about Nathan Rivers or something about your father, he will believe us."

"I hope so," Andrea said. She looked at Sara and smiled. "If we are to go shopping, then I need to take a shower."

"Right," Sara agreed. "And I need to change clothes. I'll meet you downstairs when you're finished."

Andrea nodded as she pulled back the covers. She got out of bed and headed for the bathroom, humming a soft tune.

***

Adam couldn't remember a single word he was reading in the newspaper. His mind was playing back the events of the previous night. He had been angry when Carol had shown up and dropped her bombshell.

He'd had every intention of getting Andrea to tell him the truth when he went looking for her last night, but when he'd found her soaking wet and crying, he couldn't bring himself to question her.

He knew when he'd taken her upstairs, he should have turned around and walked out. But, he couldn't do that either. Her soft plea for him to stay had been his undoing. He had wanted her more than he had ever wanted any other woman and they had made love throughout the night.

But in the cold light of day, he knew he had to talk to her, needed for her to tell him the truth.

When she came downstairs a short time later, he was prepared with the questions he wanted to ask her.

However, the words he was about to say died on his lips when she walked through the door. The soft look in her eyes and the smile on her lips took his breath away.

He shook his head to clear the cobwebs from his mind. "Andrea, we need to talk," he began, but before he could get another word out, a loud squeal came from the foyer and a moment later, Daniel came in holding his Uncle's hand.

He heard Andrea's gasp and looked sharply at her. Her face had turned ashen at the sight of his brother. Did she know him? Had his theory about her traveling through time been a mistake?

"What are you doing here?" Adam asked, dragging his gaze from Andrea to his brother.

"What, no hello?" his brother returned.

Adam looked down at his son. "Go outside and play, Daniel."

"Ah, can't I stay?" Daniel whined.

"Now," Adam said quietly. Daniel pouted, but did as he was told.

"Why are you here, Nate?" Adam asked.

"It's nice to see you too, brother," Nate stated dryly. "Well, who do we have here?" he asked, looking Andrea up and down.

Adam scowled at the look in his brother's eyes. "Nate, this is Andrea Marsh. Andrea, this is my brother, Nate."

"Delighted to meet you," Nate said as he took her hand and brought it to his lips.

Andrea tried to control the shudder that shook her body at the touch of his lips on her hand. She felt his hot breath and pulled her hand from his grasp and took a step back. "If you will excuse me, I will leave you two alone," she gasped.

"We need to talk, Andrea," Adam said.

"We can talk later," she whispered, backing out of the room.

"Very lovely," Nate murmured as he watched Andrea's exit.

"Again, what are you doing here, Nate?" Adam repeated his question.

Nate shrugged his shoulders. "What, I can't come home for a visit?"

"You only come home when you want something," Adam replied. "Did you run out of money? Is that why you're here?" he asked.

"So, is Andrea the new woman in your life?" Nate asked, ignoring Adam's question.

"She works here," Adam answered tightly.

"Doing what?" Nate asked, surprise evident in his voice.

"She's working with the horses."

"Oh, that's a good one!" Nate said, laughing. At the look on his brother's face, he frowned. "You're serious? She's actually working with the horses?"

"She's good at it," Adam replied tersely.

"Are you sleeping with her?" Nate asked quietly.

"How much do you need?" Adam demanded angrily, going to his desk and pulling out his checkbook. "I know that's why you're here. You've either run out of money or owe some loan shark." When Nate had turned thirty, Adam had turned his trust fund over to him to do with as he wished.

"I don't want any money!" Nate snapped.

"Then why are you here?"

"I told you, I'm here for a visit."

"How long are you planning on staying?" Adam asked.

Nate shrugged. "I don't have any place I have to be right now, so, who knows?"

Adam placed the checkbook back in the drawer and slammed it shut. "I don't want any trouble out of you, Nate," he said.

"What trouble could I possibly cause?" Nate returned, appearing to be hurt by his brother's comment.

"And stay away from Andrea," Adam warned.

"Then you are sleeping with her," Nate said quietly. Adam refused to respond. "What about Carol?"

Adam frowned. "What about her?"

"I was under the impression she would be the next Mrs. Adam Rivers."

Adam laughed harshly. "Hardly."

"Does she know that?" Nate asked, narrowing his eyes.

"My personal life is none of your concern," Adam said tightly.

Nate held up his hands in surrender. "Whatever you say, big brother. Now, if you'll excuse me, I'm going to find Catherine. I'm starving."

Adam swore softly. He and Andrea needed to talk. He needed to let her know that what had happened between them last night should not happen again. He'd had no right to take advantage of her and needed to make her understand that.

His brother's timing, as usual, sucked, and Adam felt that his return would bode nothing but trouble.

***

Andrea wasn't in the stables nor was she in her bedroom when Adam went looking for her. He found Catherine in the kitchen, making preparations for Sunday dinner and asked her if she had seen Andrea.

"I believe Ms. Marsh and Sara went to town," she told him. "You did tell Sara it was okay to go shopping," she reminded.

"Yea, I guess I forgot," he said. "Where's Nate? I thought he was coming in here to get something to eat."

"He grabbed a snack and said he wanted to take one of the horses out for a ride and that he'd be back in time for dinner."

Adam sighed. "Then, I guess I'll be in my study if anyone needs me."

He sat at his desk, sorting out the bills that needed to be paid and writing out checks for them. Andrea's face kept creeping into his mind and images of their lovemaking. He knew he should have stopped when he discovered that she was a virgin, but God help him, he couldn't. The fact that he was her first had fueled the fire in his body even more.

He scowled when he thought of her reaction to Nate. Did the two of them know each other? If his theory was correct, then there was no way that could be possible. But, if they didn't know each other, why did she have such a frightening reaction to him?

Just the thought of his brother touching her enraged him. Nate destroyed every woman he came in contact with. He'd left some women penniless, some women broken hearted and one woman dead.

He didn't want Nate anywhere near Andrea, but just because he had made love to her, did he have the right to dictate who she saw and who she didn't?

He sighed heavily and pushed away from the desk. He stuck his head in the kitchen door and told Catherine he was going to the office for a little while and would be back in time for dinner.

***

Andrea had begged off from going shopping, telling Sara she didn't feel up to discovering new gadgets and making conversation with people she didn't know. Instead, she asked Sara to go for a walk with her down by the lake.

As they left the house and cut through the woods, Sara noted Andrea's silence and asked what was bothering her.

Andrea stopped and turned to face Sara. "Why didn't you tell me about your Uncle?" she asked quietly.

Sara clamped her hand over her mouth and her eyes rounded in surprise. "Oh my God, I forgot! I am so sorry," she whispered. "I haven't seen Uncle Nate since my mother died."

"He looks a lot like Nathan, Sara," Andrea said. She started walking again and Sara fell in beside her.

"How do you know about Uncle Nate?" Sara asked, frowning.

"I met him a little while ago."

"Uncle Nate's home?" Sara asked, surprised.

"Yes, he came in while your father and I were talking."

"I wonder why he's back," Sara murmured.

"Isn't this his home?" Andrea asked.

"Yea, but when he left, he said he would never be back."

"Why?"

"I don't' know. Like I said, I haven't seen him since my mother died. Before that, he was around a lot. But then he and my father started arguing a lot and after mom died, Uncle Nate left and no one has heard from him since."

"I'm sorry, Sara."

"I had totally forgotten that Uncle Nate was named after my great, great grandfather, Nathan and that he favored him," Sara said. They had reached the lake and sat down under a big oak tree. "I can just imagine your reaction when you saw him," Sara said.

"It did surprise me. For a moment, I actually thought I was home," Andrea admitted. "What was he like when he was here?"

"He was really fun to be around. He used to take Daniel and me fishing a lot, played games with us and took us to the movies sometimes. I don't know what he's like now."

"We've never talked about your mother. How did she die?" Andrea asked quietly.

"She was thrown from her horse."

"I'm sorry."

"I had come downstairs that morning and she and my father were in his study with the door closed. I could hear them yelling at each other so I tried to listen at the door. I couldn't make out all the words, but I could tell dad was really mad because he was calling her names."

She took a deep breath and continued. "I heard something crash and started to open the door when it flew open. Mom pushed me aside and ran out the front door. I followed her and called after her, but she didn't hear me. When I turned back around, dad was going up the stairs."

"Later that night, dad came to my room and told me what had happened. It wasn't until after the funeral that I found out she had been riding too close to the cliff on the other side of the woods and something spooked her horse. She was thrown off and went over the cliff." There were tears running down her cheeks when she finished.

Andrea put her arm around her. "I am so sorry, Sara. I had no idea," she whispered.

Sara wiped the tears from her face as she pulled away from Andrea. "That was a long time ago."

"Do you blame your father for your mother's death?"

She nodded her head. "For a long time, I did," she responded. "If they hadn't been fighting, she wouldn't have run from the house."

"Your father didn't put her on that horse, Sara," Andrea said gently.

"I don't want to talk about this anymore," she said, moving away from Andrea.

"All right," Andrea agreed. "Do you mind telling me about your mother? What she was like? What she looked like?" Andrea asked her.

"She was beautiful," Sara whispered, turning back to face Andrea.

"Do you or Daniel look like her?" Andrea asked.

Sara nodded. "Daddy says I do, that I have her eyes and her smile. I know she liked to dance and loved to play the piano. Before she died, she was going to start giving piano lessons to me and Daniel."

"But that never happened?" Andrea asked quietly.

"No, she died before she got a chance to teach us."

"I'm really sorry, Sara. I know how much you miss her."

"I've been thinking about our family history," Sara said, changing the subject as she wiped the tears from her eyes. "And I think I should talk to dad and see what I can find out about his great grandfather."

"Won't he become suspicious if you start asking him questions about Nathan?"

Sara shrugged her shoulders. "I can tell him that I'm doing a family tree and need to get all the information I can get. He won't be suspicious if I ask him the right questions."

"If you think it's a good idea, then I agree."

"I really think he would believe us if we told him the truth, Andrea," Sara suggested.

Andrea shook her head. "He would think we're both crazy and send me away."

"Okay, okay, I won't tell him, but, I am going to ask him questions," Sara said sighing as she stood. "We better head back or Ms. Floyd will be upset if we're late for dinner."

"Thank you, Sara," Andrea said quietly.

They were both silent on the walk back to the house.

***

Sunday dinner was eaten in silence. Sara had greeted her Uncle with coolness, thereby setting the mood at the table.

Every so often, Andrea would secretly glance across the table at Nate. Her first look at him had startled her, but the more she looked at him, the more he resembled Adam, not Nathan. Both men had Nathan's coloring and body structure, but that was as far as it went.

Where Nathan's eyes were a cold blue, Adam's were warm and smiling, and Nate's eyes seemed to have a mischievous glint to them. She wondered silently if his personality was similar to Nathan's.

Later that evening after Daniel had gone to bed and Andrea excused herself, Sara and her father were alone in the living room. She decided this was as good a time as any to question him about their family.

"Dad, can I talk to you for a few minutes?" she asked.

"Sure, what's up?"

"I'm doing a paper on genealogy for history class and was wondering if you could help me." She hated lying to her father, but felt it necessary under the circumstances.

"What do you need to know?" Adam asked as he closed the book he had been reading.

She sat down in one of the wing chairs across from the sofa and pulled out her notebook and pen from her backpack. "Well, let's see," she began hesitantly. "Maybe we should start with your great grandfather, Nathan. What do you know about him?"

"Not much. Dad never talked much about him."

"I don't remember you ever talking about him or your great grandmother," she said. "Do you know anything about her?"

He smiled. "You were named after her; that I do know. Her name was Saralyn. We just separated yours to Sara Lynn. From what my father told me, she was a very strong willed woman."

Sara scribbled on her notepad. "Do you know how many children they had?"

"I believe there was a boy and a girl, but if I remember correctly, the girl died at an early age."

"How did she die?"

"I never learned the truth about that. All I was told was that she ran away from home when she was about sixteen and no one heard from her again until they learned of her death."

"Do you know if Saralyn was Nathan's first choice for a wife?"

Adam frowned slightly. "Now, that I don't know."

"Do you know how Nathan came to own this house?"

"I was told he built it for his wife."

"I don't think so."

"What do you mean?" Adam asked sharply.

Too late, Sara realized her mistake. "What I mean is, uh, was it possible that Nathan could have gotten this house from someone else or maybe through foreclosure at a bank or something?"

"No," Adam said shaking his head. "I'm sure he had this house built."

"Did Nathan run for any type of office, like the Senate or anything?"

Adam rubbed his chin thoughtfully. "I think I remember something about that. He was running for a Senate seat for the state of Georgia, but I think someone beat him out."

Sara finished writing and placed the notepad and pen back in her backpack.

"That's it?" Adam asked.

"Yea," she replied. "I pretty much know what happened after that. I just needed to fill in the blanks."

Did Sara know about Andrea? If he believed that Andrea had traveled through time, what did his family history have to do with it? Was it possible Andrea traveled here from the late 1800's and had known his great grandfather? The closer he got to believing she had traveled through time, the more frightened he became.

"Is there anything you want to tell me, Sara?" he asked quietly.

Sara frowned. Should she tell him? Would he believe her? She hated lying to him, but she couldn't betray Andrea. If anything were to happen to Andrea, she would never forgive herself.

"I don't think so," she finally responded to his question.

"You're sure?"

"I'm sure." She kissed him on the cheek. "Thanks for the information."

He watched her saunter from the room, sure she had wanted to tell him something, but seemed afraid to do so. He thought about her questions and wondered where she got the idea that Nathan Rivers had been in love with anyone other than Saralyn. And why would she think Nathan acquired this house by any other means than having it built?

Sara leaned against the wall outside the living room and breathed a sigh of relief. She had come too close to telling her father the truth. She loved her father very much, but didn't know if he would understand about Andrea.

What if Andrea were right? What if she had told her father truth and he'd had Andrea arrested? She couldn't do it. She couldn't let Andrea be taken from her.

Chapter 9

*A*t about the same time Adam and Sara were having their discussion on family history, Nate was meeting with the person responsible for his return to Savannah.

"It took you long enough," Carol snapped when she opened the door to let Nate in.

Nice to see you too," Nate replied dryly.

"Have you seen Adam yet?" she asked.

Nate nodded his head. "My big brother wasn't happy to see me."

"I don't imagine he was," she said. "You two didn't exactly part on good terms."

"Adam just holds a grudge longer than I do, that's all."

"Did he happen to fill you in on what's been going on?"

He shook his head. "Did you really think he would?" Nate returned.

Carol told him what had taken place up until yesterday. When she had finished, Nate laughed softly.

"It's not funny!" she snapped.

"Sounds to me like you're losing what little hold you think you have on Adam," he said.

"I'm not losing anything," she replied. "Adam has just been a little distracted lately, that's all."

"I'd say Ms. Marsh is a very nice distraction."

"She's a liar and an imposter," Carol said coldly.

"Just what is it you want me to do?" Nate asked.

"I want you to get rid of her."

"And how do you propose I do that?" he asked, raising an eyebrow.

"You took care of Amanda, didn't you?" she asked sweetly.

"Amanda was thrown from her horse," he said, his eyes narrowing.

"If memory serves me correctly, you were the reason she and Adam were fighting in the first place, causing her to race off on her horse."

"But I didn't kill Amanda and I'm not going to kill Andrea Marsh," he told her coldly.

"I don't want you to kill her," Carol said, sighing. "I just want you to get her out of the way."

"How?" he asked.

"Women succumb to your charms, Nate. Surely you can come up with something to lure her away from Adam."

"You're really scared of her, aren't you?"

"I'm not scared of her!" she grated harshly. "You know Adam is always for the underdog. He's most likely mistaking pity for attraction."

"He's already slept with her, you know," Nate said quietly.

"He told you that?" she whispered, her face ashen.

"He didn't have to," Nate replied. "He just told me to stay away from her."

Carol waved her hand in dismissal. "That doesn't mean he's slept with her," she said, relief in her voice. Nate shrugged, but didn't respond.

"Look, I really need your help on this, Nate," she said.

"What's in it for me?" he wanted to know.

"You can have Andrea, if you want her."

"What if she doesn't want me? What then?"

"You took Amanda away from Adam; surely you won't have any trouble taking Andrea away as well."

***

Andrea didn't come down for dinner the following evening, telling Sara that she had a headache, so Sara took a tray up to her.

When Andrea didn't answer the door after several knocks, Sara took the tray back downstairs.

Nate had still not returned, so Adam, Sara and Daniel had dinner alone.

After they had finished dinner, Daniel went in to watch television and Sara went to her room, saying she had some studying to do for an exam at school tomorrow.

Adam tried watching television with Daniel, but couldn't get interested in anything that was on. He tried going through his paperwork, but couldn't concentrate on that either. So, at eight o'clock, he told Daniel it was time to go to bed and he too went upstairs.

He stopped in front of Andrea's door and knocked lightly. When there was no answer, he turned the knob and opened it. He found the room empty and was about to go back out when he heard water running. He closed the door and locked it.

Andrea gasped when she walked out of the bathroom a few minutes later and saw Adam sitting on her bed. "How did you get in here?"

"The door was unlocked," he replied. "We need to talk, Andrea," he said quietly.

"Can't this wait until tomorrow?" she asked, clutching the towel wrapped around her.

"No, it can't," he replied, his voice husky with the desire he was already experiencing at seeing her body wrapped in a towel. Her skin was still pink from the hot shower and water glistened on her body where the towel didn't cover her.

"Adam, please," she whispered imploringly.

"How do you know my brother?" he asked, ignoring her plea.

"I don't know your brother!" she replied, shocked at his question.

"Then why did you act the way you did when you saw him this morning?"

"He reminded me of someone, that's all," she replied vaguely.

"Who?"

"I've never met your brother before today, Adam," she replied, evading his question.

"I think you're lying," he said quietly.

"How would I know him?" she countered. "According to Sara, he's been gone for some time, so how could I possibly know him?"

She was right. Nate had been gone for a while and before that, he was only here for a short time. But it was possible that they had met some place else. "Then, what are you not telling me?" he asked instead. He wanted her to tell him the truth.

She walked over to the dresser and picked up the brush and began pulling the tangles from her hair.

Adam walked up behind her and grabbed her hand in mid air. "Why won't you tell me?" he whispered against her hair.

Her breath caught in her throat at his nearness. Unable to speak, she shook her head.

"Do you think I will make you leave if you tell me the truth?" he asked softly. "I won't do that, I promise."

She turned and looked up at him, tears forming in her eyes. "I can't," she whispered brokenly.

The feel of her body against his sent hot flashes throughout his body. Without thinking, he brought his mouth down hard on hers, pulling on the sweetness within.

She moaned softly as her body melted into his. The towel came loose and fell at her feet.

Adam picked her up and carried her to the bed. He quickly removed his clothes and slid on top of her. He entered her with one swift thrust, causing her to cry out in surprise.

She wrapped her legs around his waist and hugged him tight as wave after wave crashed upon her.

He stiffened with his release as they crested together.

He slid off her and lay on his back, breathing hard. A few minutes later, he got up and put his clothes on. Without saying a word to her or even looking at her, he left.

Andrea wiped the tears from her eyes as she crawled off the bed. She took a gown from the dresser drawer and slipping it over her body, got back in bed and cried herself to sleep.

Adam berated himself for his treatment of Andrea as he removed his clothes and crawled into his own bed.

He had been angry because she wouldn't confirm his suspicions and continued to lie to him. But that was no excuse for his taking her so coldly.

He could still feel the touch of her body on his as he turned out the light and pulled the covers over him.

Chapter 10

*T*he next few days went by quickly for Andrea. She was up before dawn each morning and worked with the horses until noon when she would go in for lunch.

Some days when Sara and Daniel came home from school, they would do their homework then would sit on the fence and watch Andrea. Other days, the children would go to a friend's house or stay after school for some social event and she wouldn't see them until dinner.

The three of them usually ate dinner together because Adam worked late, not coming home until after everyone had already gone to bed.

She hadn't seen Nate since his return and wondered if he had left town again. No one seemed to know where he spent his days and nights.

During her trips into the house during lunch, she and Mrs. Floyd became friends. She learned quite a lot about Adam and his family from their conversations.

On one such occasion, Mrs. Floyd told her about Adam's father, Randolph Rivers, who had started the advertising company that Adam was now president and CEO of.

Apparently, Randolph had loved his youngest son very much, but didn't trust him, so he had left everything to Adam with the stipulation that Adam would take care of Nate. This had caused problems between the brothers, so shortly after Randolph's death, Nate had left, coming back for only brief periods of time.

The last time he came home had been three years ago, deciding that he wanted to help Adam run the business. Adam was happy because he thought it would help mend the differences between them.

Mrs. Floyd told Andrea that the separation between Adam and Nate had something to do with Amanda, Adam's wife.

According to her, the months prior to Amanda's death, Adam and Nate fought constantly. Mrs. Floyd had discovered that Amanda and Nate had been having an affair and that Adam had found out.

The night Amanda died, she and Adam had been arguing about her affair with his brother. Amanda had informed him she wanted a divorce so she could be with Nate and Adam refused, telling her he would not allow her to leave the children.

Andrea knew nothing about Nate, but she couldn't imagine any woman choosing him over Adam.

Andrea's thoughts were constantly on Adam. She knew she was in love with him and it pained her to know he didn't return the feeling. Their first night together had been beautiful and Andrea had learned what it was to truly love someone.

However, the last time he made love to her was something she wished to forget. Adam had been angry with her and had been cold and unfeeling, and she guessed the reason he didn't come home at night was because he felt repulsed and couldn't stand the sight of her.

She knew if she had another place to go, she would leave his home, never to return, no matter how much it hurt.

So, to keep her mind occupied, she turned her entire attention on training Adam's horses and spending as much time with Sara and Daniel as she could.

***

He stood at the entrance, watching her silently as she talked softly to Max.

Andrea felt a presence and turned around and glared at the man standing in the doorway. "It's not polite to sneak up on someone," she said.

"I wasn't sneaking," Nate said as he walked over to where she stood. "You were so engrossed in what you were doing; you obviously didn't hear me come in." She didn't respond as she continued rubbing Max down.

"Adam said you were very good at what you do," he commented. "Where did you learn so much about horses?"

Andrea stiffened as she moved away. "From my father," she replied.

"Did he have a lot of horses?"

"He had one of the largest horse ranches in the county."

"Really? And where was this?"

She realized too late that he was trying to trick her. "Ah,"she stammered, "you wouldn't have heard of it."

Nate shrugged. "I've been all over the world. It's quite possible I've heard of it."

"It doesn't matter. My father isn't there anymore."

"Is your father dead?" he asked quietly.

Andrea felt the sting of tears at the back of her eyes. "Yes," she replied softly.

"I'm sorry," Nate said. He walked over and opened the stall door for her and waited until she walked Max in and came back out. "How did you end up here?" he asked.

"It's a long story."

Nate spread his arms wide, smiling. "I've got nothing but time."

"Well, I don't," she said. She tried to pass him when he grabbed her by the arm.

"What's going on between you and Adam, Andrea?"

"I don't remember giving you leave to use my name," Andrea stated as she jerked her arm from his grasp.

"When I walked in on you two the other day, I could tell something was going on. Have you slept with him yet?" he asked softly.

"I don't think that's any of your damn business," Adam said coldly as he entered the stable.

Adam's reasons for not going home weren't because he couldn't stand the sight of Andrea. It was because he was ashamed of how he'd treated her. He fought his feelings for her every day but knew he was losing the battle. He knew he was falling in love with her and the thought of her lying to him made him lose all reasoning.

He knew he had to apologize for his behavior and deciding to do just that, he had left his office with the hopes of mending the gap between them.

At this time of day, he knew where he would find Andrea, so he parked his car and went directly to the stables. Just as he was about to walk through the stable doors, he heard his brother's voice, and decided to stand outside to see what his brother was up to. When he heard Nate's last question, he entered the stables.

He could tell by the look in Andrea's eyes that she was frightened of Nate.

"Adam," she breathed in relief.

"Thought you'd left town," Adam said to Nate.

"Why would you think that?" Nate returned.

Adam shrugged. "No one has seen you around for a few days," Adam replied.

"Just taking care of some business and getting re-acquainted with old friends," Nate said.

"If you will excuse us, Andrea and I need to discuss some business," Adam told Nate.

"Horse business?" Nate inquired, smiling softly.

"Right," Adam replied. Nate stood there, staring at Andrea. "*Now*, please?" Adam insisted quietly.

As soon as Nate left, Adam turned to Andrea. "Are you all right?" She shook her head. "He really frightens you, doesn't he?"

"I don't know why," she replied, her voice shaky, "There's just something about him that seems to scare me," She laughed nervously.

Adam laughed harshly. "I know my brother and I've seen him evoke a lot of things in women, but I've never known fear to be one of them."

Her conversation with Mrs. Floyd about Nate and Amanda flashed across her mind. "You said you had some business to discuss with me," she said stiffly.

"Actually, I wanted to apologize for my behavior the other night," he said quietly. "I was angry because I thought you were lying to me about Nate."

"I wasn't," she said.

"I know that now. But when I thought about you in my brother's arms…"

"Never!" Andrea responded fiercely.

"I really am sorry, Andrea."

"You truly didn't mean to hurt me the way you did?" she whispered.

"What happened that night should never have happened and I promise it will never happen again."

Andrea frowned. "You mean you won't make love to me again?" she queried softly.

Adam laughed lightly and ran a finger down the side of her face. "I mean that I won't ever hurt you again," he whispered.

"Then, I accept your apology," she said, smiling.

"Thank you," he responded. "Now, how would you like to go out to dinner with me tomorrow night?"

"Go out to dinner? You mean to a restaurant?"

"Yes, to a restaurant," he replied, smiling.

"I can't."

"Why not?" he asked, frowning.

"I promised Sara I would go mall shopping with her."

"I'm sure Sara won't mind going Saturday instead of tomorrow evening," he said, smiling.

"I really don't want to go to a public place, Adam," she said quietly.

"Want to tell me why?" he asked, frowning slightly.

"I just don't think I can be around a lot of people I don't know. I would be nervous and neither one of us would enjoy the evening." Not to mention that she wouldn't know how to act in a restaurant in this time, she thought silently.

He sighed. She wasn't going to tell him. "Then, how about dinner alone with me here?" he suggested.

"I'd like that," she replied, smiling in relief.

"How's eight o'clock sound?"

"Eight o'clock is fine," she agreed.

***

"Where have you been?" Carol asked Nate as he strolled into her apartment later that afternoon.

"I've been busy," he replied.

"So, have you made any progress with Ms. Marsh?"

"Would you be a dear and pour me a drink?" he asked, sitting down in one of the chairs next to the fireplace.

She poured two glasses and handed one to him. "Well?"

He thought back to his conversation with Andrea. "Some," he replied vaguely. "Tell me what your investigation turned up."

"The only information I have is on an Andrea Marsh who disappeared around eighteen eighty-nine. According to some old newspaper clippings, her body was never found so she was presumed dead," Carol replied, sitting in the other chair across from him.

She took a sip of her drink and leaned back in the chair. "What I think you might find interesting is that she was somewhat connected to your family."

"How so?" he asked, his interest piqued.

"The newspaper clipping made reference to her impending marriage to your great grandfather, Nathan Rivers."

"That is interesting," Nate murmured.

"This woman, whoever she is, must have thought that no one would suspect anything and just took Andrea Marsh's identity."

Nate was frowning hard and Carol could see that he was thinking about something. "What are you thinking?" she asked.

"I was just wondering why she would go to all that trouble."

"Because she's a con artist," Carol snapped.

"I don't think so," Nate murmured. "You can tell by her manner and speech that she's educated and the way she carries herself speaks of breeding."

"You're falling for her!" Carol accused fiercely.

"Don't be ridiculous!" Nate snapped.

"Why is it that you and your brother always seem to have the same taste in women?" she asked, disgust in her voice. She shook her head and took another sip of bourbon. "I think I'm the only one you two have different opinions about," she added.

"Oh, I wouldn't say that. I believe Adam and I often have the same opinion about you," he said, a small smile playing at the corner of his mouth.

Carol smiled sweetly at him, taking the meaning of his words as a compliment. "What are you going to do about her?" she asked.

Nate finished his drink and set the empty glass down on the coffee table. "I think I'm going to get to know *this* Andrea Marsh a little better," he replied.

"Just keep me informed of your progress," Carol told him as he was leaving.

Nate sat outside in his car for several minutes replaying his conversation with Andrea over and over in his mind.

She'd said her father owned a horse ranch in Savannah and that he was dead. He knew most everyone around here and had never heard of any rancher named Marsh. Then, there was the part about her not giving him leave to use her name. What was that about? he wondered.

The thing that bothered him the most however, was her apparent fear of him. They'd never met, so why would she be afraid of him? Why did she freak out every time she saw him? The first time they met, she had acted like she'd seen a ghost and had fled as quickly as she could.

Suddenly, a thought struck him. Could it be possible? He'd heard of this sort of thing before, but never actually knew of it happening.

His frowned deepened as he shifted the car into drive and pulled away from the curb.

***

"You look lovely," Adam told her as he poured two glasses of wine.

"Thank you," Andrea responded, blushing as she took a sip of hers. "Are the children in bed?" she asked.

"Getting ready," he replied. "I'll go up in a little while and say good night."

They were silent as they began eating the dinner Mrs. Floyd had prepared for them before retiring for the evening. "Will you tell me about your wife? What was she like?" Andrea asked quietly. When she saw him stiffen, she added, "if it's too painful, you don't have to."

He smiled as he shook his head. "I met Amanda in college and we became good friends. She was very shy and had a hard time meeting people."

He smiled at the memory as he continued. "We started doing everything together, studying, going to movies, that sort of thing. Eventually, our friendship turned into love. At least that's what we thought it was."

"After we graduated, we got married and I went to work with my father while Amanda started working for a small accounting firm."

"She worked outside the home?" Andrea asked, surprised.

Adam frowned. "She went to college to become an accountant. Anyway, shortly after we got married, she became pregnant with Sara. I don't think Amanda was ready for a child because for a long time after Sara was born, she spent very little time with her. She was working hard to become a partner in her firm and worked long hours. And since I was trying to learn the marketing business, I wasn't home much either."

"Is that when you hired Mrs. Floyd?" she inquired.

"Yes," he replied, smiling. "Catherine has been a blessing to this family. She has taken care of all of us for a long time."

"I can't imagine any woman not wanting a child," Andrea said softly.

"Amanda did want children, but just not so soon," he said. "That's why I was surprised when she got pregnant with Daniel. At first, she was upset about the pregnancy, and then she changed and seemed to be happy about it. She cut back her hours at work and after Daniel was born she spent more time at home with both children."

"Sara told me about the accident. It must have been devastating for you," she said quietly.

A look of anger flashed in his eyes for a moment that startled Andrea. "It was devastating for all of us," he responded. "What about you?" he said, changing the subject. "I overheard you telling Nate that your father was a horse rancher?" Maybe if he got her on the subject, she would open up to him.

"Yes, he is, was, and a much respected one," she replied. It was hard for her to refer to her father as if he were dead, but in this time, he was.

"He's the one who taught you how to work with horses?" Adam asked.

She nodded her head. "I helped with getting them ready for shows and auctions. Before my mother died, she and my father worked together and they both taught me. Then, after she died, I did most of it myself."

"How did your mother die?"

"I was told she had a weak heart," Andrea replied quietly. "Anyway, my father didn't handle her death very well and began drinking and gambling."

"Is that why you never married?"

She thought about Nathan for a moment and shrugged her shoulders. "There was one man who thought I would marry him, but as you can see, it never came to pass."

"Is that why you left home? Because you didn't want to marry this man?"

Andrea realized that if the conversation continued on this path, she would end up telling him everything. "Did you not say you were going up to say good night to the children?" she asked.

Adam sighed as he pushed away from the table. She still didn't trust him. "Yes, I did," he replied, noting her subtle way of changing the subject. "I'll be back in a few minutes."

Andrea released the breath she had been holding as she got up from the table. She walked over to the window and stared out at the night. She had almost told Adam that she was from the past! What was she thinking? It must be the wine, she thought. She wasn't used to drinking and it must have gone straight to her head.

She wanted to tell him, wanted desperately to ask him to help her get back home. Or did she? If she could get back, would she want to leave Adam and the children now that she had come to love them?

"I must say, you fill that dress out a hell of a lot better than Amanda ever did," Nate said as he walked in.

Andrea stiffened and turned to face him. "Does Adam know you're here?" she asked.

"I wasn't aware that I had to report to my brother every time I came home," he replied dryly.

"That's not what I meant," Andrea said, frowning.

"Why are you frightened of me, Andrea?" he asked.

"I'm not frightened of you," she replied stonily.

"Yes, you are," he said. "I would never hurt you. All I want is to be your friend."

"Why?" she asked, looking directly into his eyes. "You don't know anything about me, so why would you want to be my friend?"

"I know more than you think I do," he replied softly.

"Such as?"

"Such as your appearance here during a thunderstorm and your apparent memory loss: such as the fact that you're using a dead woman's identity."

"I gather you've been talking to Carol," she said stiffly.

Nate shrugged. "She seems to be the only one to bring me up to date on what's been happening around here since I've been gone. She truly believes that you are an imposter."

"That's a lie!" she cried angrily.

"Nate, so good of you to grace us with your presence, *again*," Adam said dryly entering the room.

"Do you have some sort of radar or something?" Nate asked, laughing.

"Did you need to see me?" Adam asked.

He looked around and noticed the burning candles on the table and the empty wine glasses. "I see I've interrupted your evening. I do apologize. We can talk later," he looked at Andrea and winked. "You two kids have fun."

"I'm sorry about that," Adam said.

"Don't apologize for your brother," she said quietly.

"I thought by now he would have grown up."

She turned back to the window and crossed her arms at her waist. Adam came up behind her and slipped his arms around her. She sighed softly as she leaned her head back against his chest.

"You didn't seem afraid of him this time," he murmured against her hair.

"Must be the wine," she returned, smiling. He turned her around in his arms and kissed her tenderly. She wrapped her arms around his waist and returned his kiss.

"Are we going to make love now?" she whispered.

Adam couldn't recall the time he had hungered for a woman this much. Just thinking about the closeness of her body, remembering the shapely slant of her waist, hips, and the descent to her thigh made every muscle in his body ache for her.

He chuckled softly as he pulled her tight against his body. In answer to her question, he took her hand in his and they walked quietly up the stairs.

Chapter 11

*S*aturday morning, Andrea and Sara went to the mall while Adam took Daniel fishing.

Andrea was amazed at the many shops in the complex as they went into each one. She refused to accept any money from Sara and if she purchased anything, she used the money she had earned. On the drive to town, Sara had explained to her how much each bill and coin represented and how much she had to spend.

She had been frightened at all the people walking around when they first arrived, but when she realized they weren't paying her any attention, she relaxed and enjoyed herself.

Three hours later, Sara dragged her away from a window showing a display of leather pants and platform shoes. "You don't want those, trust me," Sara said.

"I don't want them. I was just wondering how anyone could walk in them."

Sara giggled. "Men and women wore them about twenty years ago and now they're back in style."

"Here," Sara said, spying the store she wanted. "We'll find something in this place."

They walked into the Gap.

An hour later, they walked out carrying new jeans and light cotton shirts for Andrea. They had even purchased a lightweight jacket for her.

They ate lunch at one of the restaurants in the food court and Andrea was amazed at all the food counters. She was so confused by all the types of foods that Sara had to order hamburgers for both of them.

"Tell me what has survived. Beyond buildings… what has survived in this time?" Andrea said, as they sat down at one of the small round tables in the middle of the food court.

"I wish I could say only the good survived, but that wouldn't be true. Generations have brought with them some of those same things that you dealt with in your time, I'm sure. Greed: arrogance. That stuff we all wish would just go away, so everybody could be happy for a change. But there's a lot of good too. Maybe you just have to look a little harder in this time, but you'll see it. You'll recognize it. I don't know that it could change."

"That's comforting to know," Andrea murmured. "Would you explain this war I read about in one of your newspapers?"

"What war?"

"All this reporting of murders across the country; I read stories and statistics and I was wondering if this country is at war again."

Sara could only stare at her. It would probably seem that way to someone from her time. "I guess you could say it's an undeclared war," she murmured.

"That must be why I haven't seen anyone in uniform," she stated.

"I don't know how to explain this, but guns are everywhere and no one knows what to do about it."

"I have no fondness for guns myself, but my father did teach me how to use one for hunting."

"I wish that's all that they were used for," Sara said.

"How old are you, Sara?"

"I'm almost thirteen."

"You seem to know a lot for someone so young," Andrea said quietly.

"Kids grow up fast in this day and time. They don't have any choice," she replied, smiling. "What was it like growing up in your time?" she asked.

"Being an only child, I was quite pampered," she replied, smiling. "My parents loved me very much and were very protective."

"Did you have many boyfriends?"

"Boyfriends? You mean, did I have a lot of gentlemen callers?" At Sara's nod, she shook her head. "I was too interested in horses and the boys didn't want to have anything to do with a girl who smelled of manure."

Sara giggled. "So, you weren't in love with anyone?"

"I never knew what love was until…"

"Until when?"

Andrea sighed heavily when she realized she had almost said until she had met Adam. Instead she said, "Until I got older and saw how much my parents loved each other."

"What happened to your mother?"

"She died three years ago, well three years ago in my time."

"I'm sorry," Sara said. "I bet you miss her."

"Very much; just as you miss your mother," she said, smiling softly. "At least you still have a father that loves you very much."

"Not until you came," Sara said quietly.

"What do you mean?" Andrea asked, frowning slightly.

"Daniel and I hardly ever saw Dad. He was always working or going out. But since you got here, he's changed. He laughs more and seems to be interested in what Daniel and I have to say or do."

"I don't know that I have anything to do with that," Andrea said. "Maybe it just took your father a little while to get over his grief."

"Maybe," Sara murmured. "Oh, by the way, I did ask him about Nathan," Sara told her.

"What did he say?" Andrea asked.

"Nothing that we didn't already know, except dad believes Nathan built our house for his wife."

"That's not true," Andrea said quietly.

"I know," Sara said. "Anyway, we'll find out more when we go back to the library."

While they were eating, Sara called Wes and told him to pick them up in front of the mall in thirty minutes.

When Wes arrived, Sara asked him to drive them to the library.

When they arrived at the library, they went directly to the room where the microfilm was stored.

Sara found the microfilm that dated back to the 1800's and after scrolling down for several minutes, located her great, great grandfather, Nathan Rivers.

They discovered that Nathan had married Saralyn the year after Andrea's disappearance. Andrea was surprised by this information. Saralyn's family was one of the wealthiest ones in Georgia, so, why had she married Nathan? Had her disappearance brought Nathan and Saralyn together? Had they comforted each other and eventually fell in love?

It was a marriage that lasted over forty years and produced two children, Nathan, Jr. and Elizabeth. It recorded their births and deaths and the names and births of their children. Adam's father, Randolph was the only son of Nathan Jr., and there was no mention of Elizabeth having had any children due to the fact that she had died in her teens.

They went to the area of the library that was called the "morgue", where old newspaper articles were also kept on microfilm. Sara ran across the article she had found when they were here before about Nathan running for the Senate and as she searched further, found another article that brought sudden tears to her eyes.

It was an article about Andrea and the night of her disappearance. "Andrea, I think you might want to take a look at this," Sara said quietly.

Andrea began reading the article and as she continued reading, tears formed in her eyes.

'The disappearance of Andrea Marsh has saddened the small town of Savannah, Georgia. Her father, Jonathan Marsh, reports that the last time he had seen his daughter was the night she disappeared. The two had dinner together and had retired for the night. When the housekeeper reported to Mr. Marsh that it did not seem that Ms. Marsh had slept in her bed the night before, the authorities were brought in and an investigation was underway. The only clue found near the edge of the cliff on the Marsh property was a shoe that Mr. Marsh said that his daughter had been wearing the night before. The authorities suspected that Ms. Marsh had been kidnapped, but when no ransom demand was made, concluded that she must have fallen into the lake and drowned or somehow wandered too close to the edge of the cliff. However, after weeks of investigation, Ms. Marsh's body still has not been recovered.

Ms. Marsh had been engaged to Mr. Nathan Rivers, C.E.O. and owner of Rivers National Bank, when she disappeared. Mr. Rivers was not available for comment.'

Andrea wiped the tears from her eyes when she finished reading. Sara hit the print button on the machine and printed a copy of the article. Folding it up, she placed it in her bag. Neither one of them spoke as Sara scrolled down and found another article.

'Mr. Nathan Rivers to marry Saralyn Flanders on April 12th. The couple will reside in the former home of Jonathan Marsh. As you may recall, Mr. Rivers was engaged to Mr. Marsh's daughter, Andrea, who was thought to have drowned in the lake on her property. Ms. Marsh's body has still not been recovered. Sources have it that Mr. Marsh was so devastated by his daughter's death that he sold his ranch to Mr. Rivers. Mr. Rivers has graciously asked Mr. Marsh to live in the home with he and his new bride after the wedding.'

Sara hit the print button again and printed out this article as well. "Well, now we know what happened to your father," she told Andrea quietly.

"He stole my property," Andrea said angrily. "Nathan used my father's grief to force him to sell it to him."

"But, *you* are living in your home again, with a few minor changes, of course," Sara reminded her.

"This is true," Andrea agreed. Tears formed in her eyes again and she smiled sadly at Sara. "I will never go back, will I?"

Sara could feel tears in her eyes as well and shook her head. "If you went back now, you could change what took place after your disappearance and my family would never exist." She put her arm around Andrea's shoulder and hugged her. "I don't want you to go because I would miss you terribly," she whispered.

"I would miss you too." Not to mention how much she would miss Adam.

"Come on, we should get home," Sara said, turning off the machine.

"Thank you, Sara," Andrea said, smiling.

Sara returned her smile and grabbed her hand as they left the library.

***

Adam stared at Carol in shock as he heard the words tumble from her mouth. "Have you gone completely mad?" he grated.

"Take a look at this," Carol said, thrusting the newspaper article at him. "Then tell me I'm mad."

Adam read the article and handed it back to her. "What does this prove?"

Carol sighed harshly. "It proves she's been lying to you about who she is!"

"Okay, so she borrowed some dead woman's identity, one that's been dead for over a hundred years, I might add. Who's she hurting? There's no one alive she can hurt by using this woman's name," he argued. He had no intention of sharing his beliefs with Carol. Better to let her think what she wanted to.

"I wouldn't exactly say that," Nate said.

Adam narrowed his eyes at his brother who had been sitting quietly on the sofa. "What is that supposed to mean?" he demanded.

"Adam, she's using you!" Carol said, bringing his attention back to her.

"How? She's asked for nothing except what she works for. I haven't caught her stealing the silver or running off with the family jewels," he added nastily.

"So, you're just going to let her get away with it," Carol stated coldly.

"Get away with what, Carol?" Adam asked quietly. "I don't see that she's done anything to anybody and especially not to you. And, I don't understand your obsession with this."

"I'm not obsessed!" she snapped. "I just don't want to see you and your family hurt by her."

Adam held up a hand. "Enough! If you want to continue to be welcome in this house, then I suggest you not bring this subject up again," his voice was deadly calm as he spoke the words.

Carol angrily grabbed her purse and headed for the door. "You will regret this Adam, that I promise you," she stated coldly.

Adam sighed heavily and poured himself a drink. He downed it quickly and looked at Nate. "Did you have something you wanted to say?" he asked coldly.

"Now's probably not a good time," Nate said when he heard the front door open. A moment later, Sara and Andrea entered the room.

Andrea knew something was wrong by the way Carol had driven her automobile away from the house and the stormy look on Adam's face. Without being told, she knew they had fought about her.

"So, how was your shopping trip?" Adam asked, trying to ease the tension in the room.

Sara glanced at Andrea before replying. "It was fine," she replied. "Is something wrong?" she asked.

"Nothing for you to worry about," Nate answered her. "Why don't you and I go see how Catherine is coming with dinner?" he asked her. Sara glanced at Andrea again before following Nate out of the room.

"Did you and Carol have words about me again?" Andrea asked, moving to stand in front of Adam.

"It's nothing for you to worry about," he told her, smiling softly.

"It is if I'm coming between the two of you," she said quietly.

He looked at her sharply. "Why would you think you would come between me and Carol?"

"I know that you two have been, ah, close and that you may be in love with her."

Adam laughed harshly. "Good God!" he exclaimed. "Why would you think that?"

"I know the two of you were seeing a lot of each other before I came here and I don't want to be the cause of you ending your relationship."

Adam smiled and shook his head. "I am not in love with Carol and you are not the cause of our disagreement," he said softly.

"You do not love her?" she whispered, looking up at him.

"No, I don't love her," he whispered back as he reached out his hand and gently touched the side of her face. Andrea stepped away from him when she heard voices in the foyer.

"Catherine says if we don't come eat now, she's throwing our dinner in the garbage," Nate said, sticking his head in the door. He glanced at Andrea and noted that she was blushing and silently wondered what he had interrupted. He then looked over at his brother and decided Carol had good reason to be worried. Adam was in love with this woman and she was in love with him. He was glad he had decided to stay for awhile. He couldn't wait to see how this played out.

Chapter 12

Carol was beginning to get scared. When she had taken the information to Adam, she was sure he would be furious and throw Andrea out of his house. But he had refused to acknowledge her accusations. It seemed he was beginning to care about this woman and she couldn't let that happen. She needed Adam and she needed his money.

While she sat in her apartment, nursing a bourbon, her thoughts went back to how she had gotten to this place in her life.

She'd never had to work for a living, being the only child of a very prominent attorney. She had been pampered and given everything she had ever wanted.

When she'd graduated from high school, her father arranged for her to marry the son of one of his partners in the firm, Frank Masters. Frank had been an eager young associate and would have done anything to make his father happy and to move up his position to partner as well. So, when his father advised him what marrying Carol would do for his career, he agreed.

When her parents had been killed in an airplane crash a year after her marriage to Frank, Carol had inherited everything, including her father's many debts. After the probate court had finished paying off all his debtors, there was a little over a million dollars left in the estate. The way she and Frank had lived, it didn't take long for the two of them to go through most of that.

When she'd found out Frank was having an affair, she divorced him and was able to maintain what was left of her inheritance.

When she and Frank had been married, they were invited to a lot of parties. At one of these parties, she had met Adam and Amanda Rivers. She had not been impressed with Amanda, with her southern accent and dowdy country ways. But, she was very impressed with Adam. He was good looking and most of all, loaded.

After her divorce from Frank, she continued going to parties and Adam and Amanda would always be there. She had also met Nate at one of these parties and they had become friends. They began going to parties together and going out once in a while. But she wanted Adam and set out to get him.

Nate's affair with Amanda wasn't something she had planned, but it worked to her advantage. She became Adam's confidant, someone he could talk to and count on.

After Amanda's death, she waited patiently until the right moment, and then made her move. She and Adam became lovers and she knew it was just a matter of time before she would become his wife.

That is, until this imposter showed up. Carol knew she had to find a way to put a stop to whatever was happening between this woman and Adam. She had worked too hard and too long to lose everything now.

Bringing herself back to the present, she picked up the telephone and dialed. "I need your help," she said when it was answered at the other end.

"Now?" the response came.

"Yes, now. I need you to get rid of someone for me."

"Like I already told you, I'm not murdering anyone," the guy said.

"I don't want you to kill her, just make her disappear," Carol told him.

"Disappear to where?"

"I don't care where, just get rid of her."

"It's gonna cost you big this time," he stated.

"I'm aware of that," Carol snapped.

"Okay. Where and when?"

"Meet me at Rodie's tomorrow night. I'll give you everything you need then," she hung up and began pacing.

This had to work, she told herself. She was running out of time and money.

***

Monday morning, Andrea waited until Sara and Daniel had left for school before going out to the stables.

She hummed a soft tune as she worked, her mind consumed with thoughts of Adam. She was sure that he felt the same way she did and that it was just a matter of time before he confessed his love for her.

Adam's thoughts were on Andrea as well until he was interrupted that morning by a visit from Renee Ramsey.

"Are you here to discuss the ad campaign for your gallery?" he asked Renee.

"That and your houseguest," Renee replied quietly.

"Andrea is not up for discussion," Adam stated flatly.

"I spoke with Carol the other day Adam, and she was very upset. She truly believes you're harboring a criminal."

Adam sighed. "I take it she told you about her investigation and what she found out."

Renee nodded. "Carol is worried that this woman is going to harm you and your children."

Adam laughed harshly. "Harm me and my children, how?"

Renee shrugged. "I don't know," she replied. "But, why did she show up on your doorstep using another woman's identity?"

"She has no intention of hurting me or my children, Renee," he said, ignoring her question. "She's a very kind and loving person. Sara and Daniel have come to love her and she loves them."

"Then why is she using a dead woman's identity? Why won't she tell you who she really is?" Renee insisted.

"I'm sure there's a good reason and I'm sure she'll tell me when she's ready," he answered vaguely.

"So in the meantime, you're just going to let her stay in your house?" she asked.

"What would you suggest? That I throw her out with no place to go?" he returned.

"You could find her a small apartment close by," she suggested.

"Andrea is not going anywhere," he said quietly.

"Adam..."

"This discussion is over," he stated coldly. "Now, if you want to discuss your ad campaign, then let's do it."

"You're in love with her, aren't you?" Renee inquired softly. "That's why you're not willing to let her go. That's why you don't care who she is or where she came from."

"I know we've been friends for many years Renee, but you go too far. What I do is no one else's business."

"Because we have been friends for many years is the reason I'm here, Adam. I don't want to see you hurt again."

Adam sighed heavily. "If you knew Andrea, then you would see why I can't let her go." The thought of her leaving left him with a cold feeling.

"Then, I would like to meet her," Renee said. "Why don't the four of you come for dinner this weekend," she suggested.

Adam frowned. "I don't know."

"You want me to stay out of your business. I can't do that because I care what happens to you. If you want to put my worries to rest, then let me meet her and form my own opinion."

"I'll take your invitation to Andrea. If she wants to meet you, then we'll come for dinner. If not..." he shrugged. "Now, do you want to discuss your ad campaign or not?"

She smiled as she opened her briefcase and pulled out the samples for him to see.

***

After dinner that night, Adam told Andrea about Renee and her invitation to dinner.

At the look of fear that entered her eyes, he said, "Renee and I grew up together. We're like brother and sister. She won't bite, I promise."

"This would make you happy, for me to meet your friends?" she asked quietly.

"I think you would really like Renee. She's quiet and very conservative. But if you don't want to go, we won't."

"Sara and Daniel will accompany us?"

"Renee invited all of us," he replied, smiling.

"Then I will go," she said.

He smiled and kissed her softly on the lips. "I'll go call her right now and tell her."

Sara entered the room as her father was leaving. "Where's dad going?" she asked Andrea.

"To make a telephone call," she replied. "It seems we have been invited to dinner at Mrs. Ramsey's home."

"Aunt Renee?" Sara repeated. At Andrea's nod, she said, "I love Aunt Renee. She's really cool. After mom died, she used to come get me and take me shopping and to the movies. You'll really like her."

"I hope so," Andrea said.

"Are you nervous about meeting her?" Sara asked.

"Yes, I am," she replied. "What will we talk about?" she returned. "I know very little about your world. How will I respond to questions she may ask?"

"Don't worry, I'll help you," Sara assured her. "Besides, you and Aunt Renee have a lot in common. She loves history, especially your era. So, when she starts talking about the old south, you'll fit right in," Sara added, laughing softly.

"I hope you're right," Andrea murmured.

Chapter 13

*R*odie's didn't boast an impressive facade. It had no windows, only boards nailed over where windows had once been. The only thing that indicated the nature of the establishment was a neon sign above the door that spelled out the name.

Once inside the lounge, it took several minutes for Carol's eyes to adjust to the darkness. She had been here once before, about a year ago, to meet the same man she was meeting tonight.

Once her eyes adjusted, she spotted whom she sought. He was sitting alone at the end of the bar, conversing with the bartender. She made her way over to him, ignoring the low whistles and obscene gestures made by the other gentlemen patrons in the bar.

Mike Stanton was a very good-looking man. He had blond hair and blue eyes and was built like a linebacker. His good looks and smooth talk could capture any woman's attention; but not Carol's. All her attention was centered on one man.

"Bring me a double scotch," she told the bartender as she walked over to a booth in the back of the bar and sat down.

Stanton followed and slid into the booth across from her. "So, who is it you want me to make trouble for?"

Carol waited until the bartender had brought her drink and left before responding. "She claims to be

Andrea Marsh, but that isn't her real name." She explained how Andrea had stolen a dead woman's identity and how she had wormed her way into Adam's household.

"Adam is thinking with his cock instead of his brain as far as this woman is concerned. He truly believes she is no threat to him."

"Just what is it you want me to do?"

"I want you to accompany me on an expedition. Nate was supposed to do it for me, but he's gone soft on me."

Who the hell is Nate?"

"Adam's younger brother," she replied. "The two of them hate each other and I thought it would be a good way for Nate to get back at Adam for stealing the business after their old man died."

"Are you talking about Adam Rivers?" Stanton asked quietly.

"Yes. Why, do you know him?"

He knew Adam Rivers quite well. The two of them had gone to high school together and played football together. They had done everything together, even screwed the same girls. They had been friends until their junior year at college, when a very pretty girl named Cindy had come between them.

Stanton had met Cindy Harrell and had instantly fallen in love with her. What he wasn't aware of was that Adam had been dating her at the same time.

When Adam found out how Stanton felt about her, he dumped her, thinking that was what his friend would have wanted. He liked Cindy, but wasn't serious about her, so he had no problem letting her go.

Unfortunately, she did. She had been in love with Adam and when he told her he thought they shouldn't see each other anymore, she became depressed and withdrawn and one day, ended her life.

Stanton had blamed Adam for Cindy's death. They had argued violently and their friendship had ended.

Through the years, he had kept track of Adam. He knew when he had married and how many children he had. He knew when old man Rivers had died, leaving everything to Adam, including the advertising business. Stanton had vowed revenge on Adam for Cindy's death, and now, it seemed that day had finally come.

"Let's just say we've met and leave it at that," he finally said. "This woman must be very important to Adam."

"She's not that important!" Carol snapped.

"Then, why would you want her out of the way?"

"She's an obstacle and I don't like obstacles," Carol replied coldly. "Are you going to help me or not?"

Stanton shrugged. "What's your plan?"

She smiled sweetly and told him what she wanted him to do. "All you need to do is hide so she can't see you and when I give you the signal, you come out and take her away."

"How long do you want me to keep her?"

"Just long enough for me to convince Adam that she ran off, taking with her certain items from his house, of course."

"You have the cash with you?"

Carol pulled an envelope from her handbag and handed it to him. "That's the down payment. You'll get the rest when the job is finished."

Stanton made no reply as he took the envelope and put it in his coat pocket.

Carol stood and looked sharply at him. "I'm counting on you so don't screw this up."

Stanton made no reply as she made her way to the door. He watched her walk away, a smile playing at the corners of his mouth. He wasn't concerned with her threat. His only concern was getting the rest of his money and finally getting back at Adam.

He thought back to the first time he had met Carol Masters about a year ago in this same bar when he had come in and found her fighting off the advances of some drunk.

He couldn't figure out why a classy lady like her would be in a place like this until he'd rescued her from the drunk and ended up at her place later. He'd discovered she wasn't the classy lady she portrayed herself to be. He'd never found out why she'd been in Rodie's that night.

He shook his head and downed his drink, waving to the bartender as he left the bar.

***

Neither Carol nor Mike Stanton was aware of the man sitting in the booth behind them, trying to listen to their conversation.

Nate had pulled up in front of Carol's apartment building just as she was driving out and decided to follow her. He was surprised when she turned into the parking lot of Rodie's.

He had followed her inside and watched as she walked over to the man sitting at the end of the bar and motioned for him to follow her. He'd been totally shocked when he saw that it was Mike Stanton.

He knew the story of what had happened between Adam and Mike Stanton and how Mike had left town shortly after Cindy's death. No one had seen or heard from him since.

So, why was he back? And how did Carol know him? Were they romantically involved? He didn't think that was the case, so then why would she meet him in a dive like this? Was Carol trying to enlist Mike's help in her quest to get rid of Andrea?

He didn't have any answers, not yet; he only knew that Carol hooking up with Mike Stanton was trouble.

He waited until Stanton followed Carol from the bar before he went out and got in his car.

He knew he had to inform Adam of what was going on and what Carol might be up to, but he needed to know for sure. The first thing he needed to do was talk to Andrea and see if his hunch about her was right.

***

It was several days later before Nate found the chance to talk with Andrea alone. He watched from his bedroom window as she made her way to the stables. He caught her just as she was about to take Max out of his stall.

"May I come in?" he asked, standing in the doorway. He didn't want her to accuse him of sneaking up on her again. She nodded her assent and he was relieved to see that she didn't appear frightened of him this time.

He walked over and sat down on a bale of hay in one corner of the stable. "I know Carol has accused you of using a dead woman's identity," he said and noticed her flinch. "So," he continued, "I did some checking on my own."

"Oh? And what did you find out?" she inquired.

"Well, Carol was right about Andrea Marsh. Seems she disappeared over a hundred years ago. But what I found most interesting is that she was engaged to my great grandfather, Nathan Rivers."

Andrea sighed audibly and sat down on one of the other bales of hay across from him, knowing that she couldn't hide the truth any longer. "Andrea was not engaged to Nathan," she said quietly.

"Then what happened to her?"

"Her father gambled her away." At the look of surprise on his face, she smiled. "You see, Jonathan, Andrea's father, thought he had Nathan Rivers beat at a game of cards. So Nathan made a wager that if he won, he would have Andrea as his wife. If Jonathan won, he would walk away with clear title to his ranch and the one next to his."

"Unfortunately for Andrea, Jonathan lost the wager and when he told her she had to marry Nathan, she became furious. They argued and she ran from the house and never returned."

"So she did drown," he surmised.

"No, she didn't drown."

"So, what happened to her?" Nate asked, frowning.

"You're looking at her," she replied softly.

"I knew it!" Nate whispered excitedly. "Time travel, right?"

"It's the only answer we've been able to come up with," she replied, nodding her head.

"We?" he asked, frowning.

"Sara and I," she replied.

"Sara," he murmured. "I should have known. She's always been too smart for her own good. How did this happen?"

Andrea explained hers and Sarah's theory of how she could have possibly traveled through time. "Sara and I believe that when I fell, I must have hit my head and that in my time, I died. It's the only explanation we can think of that could have happened."

Nate whistled softly. "So your family just found your body lying in the woods?"

Tears were beginning to form in Andrea's eyes. "No," she whispered, shaking her head. "According to the newspaper articles Sara and I found at the library, my body was never found. The authorities believed that I had fallen into the river and drowned."

"But, you didn't drown, so where's your body?"

Andrea shrugged. "That's one we haven't figured out yet."

"How about Adam? Does he know?"

"No," she replied, shaking her head.

"You're kidding, right?"

She shook her head. "I haven't found the courage to tell him."

"You mean he doesn't even have a clue?" he couldn't believe his brother hadn't figured this out yet. "He's not stupid, Andrea," he said quietly. "If I could figure it out, don't you think he's bound to, sooner or later?"

Andrea began pacing back and forth in front of the stalls. After several seconds, she turned to face him. "You're right," she agreed. "I have to tell him."

"Good," Nate said, smiling. However, his smile disappeared as he reached out and lightly touched her arm. "You need to be careful and watch your back," he warned.

"What do you mean?" she asked, confused by his words.

"I mean Carol."

Surprised, she said, "She knows about this?"

"Not about the time travel," he replied. "All she knows is that you are using someone else's identity and is hiding something, but she'll keep digging until she finds out what it is."

"Then I guess I'd better tell Adam before she does," Andrea said.

"Another thing you need to know," he continued. "Carol is very desperate. She wants Adam and will do anything to get him."

She stopped him when he reached the door. "Nate, why do you care what happens to me?" she asked.

He turned and smiled sadly at her. "I'm not as evil as everyone thinks I am," he replied softly.

Nate didn't know at what point he had changed sides. When he'd been summoned by Carol to come help her, he'd every intention of doing so. He felt she and Adam deserved each other and it was a good way to get back at his brother for all the wrong he felt Adam had done to him.

He had went after Amanda, needing to get back at Adam and finding a way of compensating for what Adam had taken from him. But he and Amanda had fallen in love and she was going to leave Adam and be with him.

When she died, he blamed Adam and vowed to make him pay. So, when Carol had offered him a way to do that, he jumped at the chance.

But in the last few days, something had changed. He wasn't sure if it was because he had finally realized Adam didn't have anything to do with Amanda's death, or if it was Andrea herself.

And as far as the advertising business went, he had finally realized that his father had been looking out for his welfare. He knew how he loved to spend money and wanted him to have a future. That's why he'd made Adam the trustee of his estate.

It seemed that Andrea's appearance in his brother's life had changed him and his children. And he was damned interested in the idea of her time traveling.

He knew now he had to keep an eye on Carol. Her desperation was real and he knew she would do anything to make sure Adam was hers.

***

Andrea was unable to find the opportunity or the courage to tell Adam that evening or the next day.

By the time she had to get ready to go to Renee's for dinner, she still had not been able to talk to him.

On the drive to Renee's home, she sat in the front seat with Adam, nervously twisting the string on the handbag that she had purchased at the mall, along with the dress and shoes Sara had helped her pick out. No matter what Sara had told her, she was afraid she would embarrass Adam.

Her nervousness was momentarily forgotten when Adam pulled into the long drive of Renee Ramsey's home. "Is Mr. Ramsey the president?" she asked in awe.

Adam smiled at the expression on her face. "No, he's just an attorney."

"I've never seen anything so beautiful," she whispered. Indeed, the governor's home in her time was not half as grand. Where the governor's home was a two-story structure and quite lovely, this home was three stories high and longer than any home she had ever seen.

The house was gray with dark green shutters and trim and the front porch covered the front of the house and wrapped around the sides. The top two floors had balconies that covered the whole front area as well. If the outside was this grand, she was sure the inside was even grander.

She was not to be disappointed. The foyer was as large as her father's study, with what looked like Italian tile covering the floor. However, very little furniture adorned this area. Two cloth-covered chairs with a small table between them were along one wall with a beautiful painting above them. On the other side, stood a long table with statues and silver plates sitting on top of it.

The woman that greeted them was a very attractive brunette, whom Andrea assumed to be Renee. She was a little taller than Andrea and her frame was small. She kissed Adam on the cheek and gave both children a hug. She then turned to Andrea.

"And you must be Andrea," she said, smiling warmly. "I'm Renee. Welcome to my home."

"Thank you," Andrea replied quietly.

Renee slapped Adam lightly on the arm. "You didn't tell me how beautiful Andrea was." Andrea blushed as Adam shrugged.

"Why don't we go into the den and have a drink. Dinner shall be ready shortly," she suggested.

"Where's John?" Adam asked as he led Andrea to the sofa.

"Adam!" John boomed as he entered the room and walked over and shook Adam's hand. "Good to see you again."

"You too, John," Adam said.

John shook Daniel's hand and bowed before Sara, who giggled. You get more beautiful every time I see you, young lady," he told her.

"Why, thank you sir," Sara grinned.

He turned to Andrea and his smile disappeared. "My wife didn't do you justice my dear. You're lovelier than she told me you were," he spoke softly as he took her hand and lightly shook it.

"Thank you," Andrea whispered, blushing for the second time that night. John Ramsey was a very handsome distinguished looking man. He wasn't quite a tall as Adam, but was about the same build. He had hazel eyes and dark brown hair, which was gray at the temples.

"John, you're embarrassing her," Renee admonished. "What would you like to drink, Andrea?" she asked.

"White wine, please," she replied.

Renee poured a glass of white wine and handed it to Andrea. "What are you drinking Adam?" He quirked and eyebrow and Renee laughed softly. "I know, scotch and water." She poured his drink and handed it to him.

"Would you two like something to drink?" she asked Sara and Daniel.

"I'll have coke," Daniel replied.

"White wine," Sara said. At the look on her father's face, she giggled. "Just kidding, dad. I'll have a coke too, please."

Everyone laughed and Andrea began to relax. Adam and John started talking and Renee sat down next to Andrea and Sara on the sofa.

"Adam tells me you are very good with horses and that you've finally broken Max," Renee said to Andrea.

"Yes," she replied. "Max is very special. I have always loved being around horses."

"How did you become involved in training them?"

"My mother and father owned several when I was young and they taught me everything they knew."

"Are your parents still alive?"

"No, they're not."

"I'm sorry. I lost my parents at a very young age and was raised by my grandparents."

"And they spoiled her rotten," Adam interjected.

Renee laughed. "You were just jealous because I got to do things you didn't get to do."

"My father would have skinned me alive if I did half the things you did."

"What did you do, Aunt Renee?" Sara asked.

"She drag raced. She skydived. She mountain-climbed," Adam answered for her.

"You skydived too," Renee said. "And if I recall correctly, you did some drag racing of your own from time to time." Everyone laughed.

"How about you, Andrea? Do any drag racing in your youth?" John asked.

Sara stiffened slightly, waiting for Andrea's response. "No, I wasn't allowed to do that," Andrea replied. She didn't know what drag racing was.

"What about, skydiving, mountain climbing, skinny dipping? Do any of that stuff?" John asked.

Andrea glanced over at Adam and found him staring at her, waiting for her response. How was she supposed to answer these questions?

Was she supposed to tell them she didn't even know what any of those things were?

Keeping eye contact with Adam, she replied, "I was an only child and my parents were very protective of me. I wasn't allowed to go anywhere they didn't go."

Adam was still staring at her, but Andrea refused to break eye contact.

"I lived a very sheltered life and was very pampered. But my parents loved me very much." She smiled at Adam before turning to face Renee. "While other children were out playing, I was being schooled at home and learning how to care for horses."

Sara squeezed her hand and smiled at her as if to say 'good save'.

Before Renee could say anything, dinner was announced.

During the meal, Renee talked with Sara about school and new movies that had come out at the theaters. Andrea listened only slightly to their conversation. She was more interested in the conversation going on between Adam and John. So enthralled with their conversation, she hardly touched the delicious meal that had been prepared.

She tried not to show her surprise and horror when they spoke of what their previous president of the United States had done while in office. Not only was she horrified that he had been sleeping with another woman, but the whole world had known about it!

Then they started talking about the wars that were taking place in some countries called Afghanistan and Iraq, places she had never heard of. It was all so frightening to her but seemed as if it were every day conversation for Adam and John.

After dinner, Adam and John went outside and Renee took Andrea on a tour of her home. She had what she called a 'play room' that she told Sara and Daniel they could go to where they could play games. Daniel happily obliged, but Sara insisted on tagging along with them.

In each room, Renee showed her several pieces of furniture that she referred to as "antiques", but to Andrea, it was what her home and others like hers were filled with.

When Renee would name a piece of furniture, Andrea would comment on it and they would launch into a discussion about it. Andrea wished to describe some of the furniture that was in her home, but knew it would bring suspicion upon herself.

They returned to the den just as Adam and John came back inside, with Daniel holding Adam's hand. "I think it's time we head home and get this sleepy head in bed," he said, looking down at his son, who was yawning.

Renee and John walked with them to Adam's car and Renee turned to Andrea. "It was really nice meeting you. I hope you will come again real soon."

"Thank you. It was a lovely evening," Andrea responded.

Renee and John stood and watched the car pull out of the driveway.

"I would say Carol has something to worry about," John said.

"What do you mean?"

"Those two are very much in love with each other."

Renee turned and kissed her husband. "You're very observant, my love," she said quietly.

***

When they arrived home, Adam took Daniel to his room and Sara followed Andrea to her room.

"You were awfully quite on the way home. Is something bothering you?" Sara asked.

Andrea sat down on the side of the bed and shook her head. "I don't know if I can make it in your world, Sara," she said quietly.

"Why do you say that? Did something happen tonight?"

"At dinner, I was listening to the conversation between your father and Mr. Ramsey. They were talking about your previous president and the things he did while in office. It was very disturbing."

"You mean about him having sex with that aide?"

"Yes, and the fact that the whole world knew about it."

Sara shrugged. "That's the media. They make everything more important than it really is."

"By media, you mean the newspapers?"

"Yes," Sara replied. "They have to sell newspapers, so they get whatever dirt they can on anyone, especially someone as important as the president."

"Then, he really didn't do the things they said?"

"He admitted to it, so I guess he did," Sara replied.

Andrea shook her head sadly. "It's very disturbing to know that the person who is supposed to oversee our country would do such a thing."

"He isn't the president anymore, so you don't have to worry about him," Sara assured her.

"Then what about this new president? I heard Mr. Ramsey tell Adam that he got us into this war with some countries called Iraq and Afghanistan. Why did you not tell me about this?"

"I'm sorry. I didn't think to tell you about it."

"Why is there a war with these countries?"

"Because terrorists crashed an airplane into one of the World Trade Center buildings."

"What is an airplane?" Andrea asked, more confused than ever.

"It's a big aircraft that flies people from one place to another."

"That's not possible!" Andrea gasped.

Sara felt the sting of tears at the horrified expression on Andrea's face. "I know all of this is scary, but in time, you will get used to it," she said softly.

"If you say so," Andrea sighed. "But why would anyone want to fly through the air in a machine?"

"Because it is a form of transportation that gets you to different cities a lot faster than riding in a car."

"Have you ever been in one of these airplanes?"

"Once, when I was seven. I went with my Mother to California to visit her Mom."

"You enjoyed it?"

"I was scared at first, especially taking off, but then it was fun."

Andrea shook her head again. "I don't know if I will ever get used to all the modern things you have in this time."

"It will take time, but I promise you, you will get used to it." She squeezed Andrea's hand and kissed her on the cheek. "I'm going to bed and I'll see you in the morning."

"Goodnight," Andrea said.

Removing the dress she had worn and the underclothes that Sara had helped her pick out, which she still was not used to wearing, she pulled on her robe and sat down at the dressing table and removed the pins holding up her hair.

A light knock came at her door and Adam entered.

"Are you all right?" he asked. "You seemed a little preoccupied on the way home."

"I'm fine," she replied, smiling. "Your friends are very nice."

"Yes, they are," he agreed, coming to stand behind her chair. "If I didn't tell you earlier, you looked very beautiful tonight," he said.

"Thank you," she murmured.

He took her hand and pulled her to her feet, facing him. "Do you know what I was thinking about all night?" he whispered.

"What?"

"How much I wanted to get you home and make love to you." His lips touched her ever so lightly and Andrea gasped at the intimate contact.

Adam reached in between them and unbuttoned her robe. When he discovered that she was naked beneath the robe, he raised his eyebrow. "I hope you were waiting for me."

"Always," she breathed just before he brought his lips to hers in a searing kiss that sent her head spinning.

He slipped the robe from her shoulders and quickly removed his own clothes. He picked her up and carried her to the bed, lying her gently down. He lay down beside her and caught her mouth in another searing kiss.

"Adam, I need to tell you something," she whispered breathlessly.

"Later," he whispered, running his hand gently up the inside of her thigh.

Andrea gasped. "Yes, later," she agreed.

Chapter 14

*S*ara found Andrea hugging tightly to the toilet the next morning. "Are you all right?" she asked.

"Being so nervous last night, I guess I didn't eat very much," she replied, as she went to the vanity and splashed cold water on her face. She placed the towel back on the rack and went into the bedroom, Sara following behind her.

"Then what you need is one of Mrs. Floyd's hearty breakfasts. Bacon, eggs…" she stopped when she saw Andrea clamp a hand over her mouth and run back to the bathroom. She stood in the doorway, watching her.

"Andrea, when was the last time you had your, ah, period?" she asked hesitantly.

"My what?" Andrea whispered.

"You know, your monthly cycle. Have you had one since you've been here?"

Andrea thought for a moment, trying to remember. "I don't think so," she replied. As understanding began to dawn on her, she let out a small gasp.

"Oh my God!" Sara breathed, a horrified expression on her face. "I'm going to kill him!" she cried. She knew it had to be her Uncle Nate who had done this to Andrea. He had raped her mother so she was sure he had raped Andrea as well.

"Sara! Wait!" Andrea yelled. Sara didn't hear her as she ran from the room.

"Oh, God, Adam!" Andrea whispered as she grabbed her robe. Slipping her arms through the sleeves, she ran after Sara.

Sara found her father in his study, reading the newspaper. "Where is he?" she demanded.

"Where's who?" Adam returned, frowning.

"Uncle Nate!" she cried. "I'm going to kill him!"

"Sara, calm down and tell me what's wrong," Adam said.

"He raped her, daddy!" she cried.

"Raped who?"

"Andrea!"

"Sara, I don't understand," Adam said.

"Uncle Nate raped Andrea and now she's pregnant!" she told him, frustration edging her voice.

The color drained from Adam's face as he looked at Andrea where she stood in the doorway. Her face was white and she was shaking her head furiously.

He looked back at Sara and took her hands in his. "Sara, Uncle Nate didn't rape Andrea," he said quietly.

"He must have, daddy," she whispered.

"If Andrea is pregnant, Sara, the baby is mine," he told her gently.

The look on her face turned to horror at his words. "How could you?! How could you take advantage of her like that?!" she cried.

Adam frowned. "Sara, Andrea and I are two consenting adults. We knew what we were doing."

"You knew what you were doing, but she didn't!" she cried. "Andrea doesn't understand how we do things here. Things were different in her time."

Adam's frown deepened at her words. "Sara…"

"How could you do such a thing!" she screamed again as she pulled her hands from his. She stopped in front of Andrea and whispered, "I'm so sorry," before running from the room.

Adam made to follow her, but Andrea halted him. "Let her go," she said quietly.

"I have to explain this to her," he said.

"Let me," she insisted.

He looked deeply into her eyes and touched her face gently with his hand. "Are you pregnant?" he asked softly.

"I could be with child," she replied.

"Why didn't you tell me?"

"Because I didn't know until a few minutes ago," she replied. "Let me go find Sara and talk to her."

"Andrea, wait," Adam said. "What did Sara mean about things being different in your time?" he asked. Would she tell him the truth now?

"We'll talk about that later," she replied. Adam sighed heavily as he watched her go.

Sara was in the backyard, sitting in one of the chairs at the picnic table. Andrea sat down opposite her and tilted her chin to look at her.

When Sara lifted her eyes to hers, tears were coursing down her cheeks. "I don't understand, Andrea. Why would daddy do that to you?" she whispered raggedly.

"Honey, your father didn't do anything I didn't want him to," Andrea said gently.

"I still don't understand. You told me than when a woman slept with a man before marriage in your time; they were labeled an outcast and considered a common woman."

Andrea flinched slightly. "I know that's what I told you and it's true. But, you told me that things like this happened every day in your world."

"Is that why you slept with him? Because you wanted to be like every other woman here?"

"I made love with your father because I love him, Sara," she replied.

Her eyes rounded in surprise. "You do?" she whispered.

"Yes, I do," Andrea replied, smiling. "I think I fell in love with him the first time I saw him and it felt right, my giving myself to him."

"Does he love you?"

"I don't know."

"What will you do if he doesn't love you?"

Andrea placed her hands lightly over her abdomen. "If I am with child and Adam doesn't want either of us, then I will have no choice but to leave."

"Where would you go? What would you do?" Sara asked worriedly.

"I guess I could find employment somewhere. I know how to train horses and I can do books. Maybe your father or Uncle would be kind enough to help me."

"Andrea, you wouldn't know how to survive in this time without me, so if you go, I go," she said, tears gathering in her eyes.

Andrea smiled. "I'm sure I could manage on my own. After all, you've taught me a lot."

"I don't want you to go," Sara whispered. "You have no idea what you mean to me."

"I hope it's the same as you mean to me," Andrea said, tears in her own eyes. "I love you, Sara."

"I love you too," she whispered, moving into Andrea's arms. Andrea hugged her tight and kissed the top of her head.

She leaned back and looked into Sara's eyes. "Why did you think that your Uncle Nate had raped me?" she asked.

Sara released herself from Andrea's arms. "Because I think he raped my mother," she replied quietly.

"Why would you think that?"

"I woke up one night because I was thirsty and was going downstairs to get something to drink. When I passed my parents room, I heard them yelling at each other. I could only make out a few words, but I heard dad say something about Uncle Nate raping her, but I couldn't hear mom's response. Then I heard dad ask her if Daniel was his son or Uncle Nate's."

"But you didn't actually hear her say that Nate raped her or that Daniel was his, did you?"

"No, but I'm pretty sure that's what she meant."

"Sara, are you all right?" Adam asked, as he walked over to where Andrea sat with her.

Sara looked up when she saw her father and shook her head, wiping the tears from her eyes.

Adam had heard what she had told Andrea and it pained him to know that she had carried this inside her all this time. He knelt down in front of her and lifted her chin. "Your Uncle Nate didn't rape your mother. He loved your mother very much."

"Then why did she say that?" Sara whispered.

"Because she was angry with me and wanted to hurt me."

"Then Daniel is your son and not Uncle Nate's?"

"Yes, Daniel is my son." he replied. Although he honestly did not know for sure if he was the biological father, by all accounts Daniel was his son.

She breathed a sigh of relief, and then asked, "What about Andrea?"

"You know I would never hurt Andrea," he replied softly.

"Then you will take care of her and the baby?"

He felt a sharp pain in his chest that she would think he would desert Andrea. "If Andrea is pregnant, I will take care of her and the baby, I promise," he glanced at Andrea then back to Sara, "Andrea and I need to talk about this. Will you leave us alone for a few minutes?"

Sara nodded and hugged Andrea again before leaving.

Adam ran a hand roughly through his hair and sighed heavily. "I had no idea she was carrying such a burden."

"Sara and I have had many conversations, but she never told me about her mother and Nate," Andrea told him. "But, I think she's going to be okay now," she assured him.

"Why didn't you tell me you were pregnant?" he asked her again.

"I honestly didn't know," she replied. "Sara found me indisposed this morning and immediately suspected that I might be with child."

He frowned slightly at her use of words and what Sara had said came to mind. "What did she mean that you didn't understand how we do things in this time?" he asked her again.

"I need to show you something," she said, knowing that now was the time to tell him. "Come with me," she told him, taking his hand. Adam frowned but followed her in the house and up the stairs.

In her room, she went over to the bedside table and took out two sheets of paper and handed them to him.

Adam glanced at them and waved them in the air. "These are copies of the same articles Carol showed me," he said.

"Carol?"

"Yes," he replied, "but I don't care that you're using the identity of a woman that's been dead for over a hundred years. I'm sure you have your reasons and you'll tell me when you're ready."

"You don't understand, Adam. I haven't stolen anyone's identity. I am Andrea Marsh."

"Then, it's true," Adam breathed, sitting down on the edge of the bed. "You really are from the past."

"You knew?" Andrea whispered. At his nod, she asked, "How?"

"I started putting the pieces together."

"Pieces of what?"

"Pieces of the puzzle," he replied, smiling. "Like your speech and how you didn't know what a television was or a video. How you evaded the questions everyone asked you and why you would use the identity of a woman that has been dead for over a hundred years. And the gown you were wearing when you arrived here," he looked up at her and added softly, "and the innocence you had each time we made love."

"Why didn't you say something?"

"At first, I was frightened by my suspicions. But when I realized it could be the only explanation, I wanted you to be the one to tell me."

"I was frightened of what you might do," she replied.

"What do you think I would have done?"

"Call the authorities and have me put away."

"I would never have done that," he told her quietly.

"I didn't know that."

"Can you tell me how this happened?"

"You already know about Sara and Daniel finding me unconscious beyond the woods," Adam shook his head and she continued. "What you don't know is how I got there."

Adam stared at her in stunned silence when she had finished her story. "Unbelievable," he whispered.

Andrea frowned. "You don't believe me?"

"No, that's not what I meant," he replied. "I mean it's a truly amazing story, but it makes more sense now."

"It does?"

"Yes. I was confused by most of the words you used and the way you acted sometimes was very strange."

"Are you saying I'm strange?" she asked, anger tinting her voice.

Adam smiled. "No, just some of the things you did were strange. For instance, the night I found you in the library going through all those books. I couldn't figure out why you would want to read history books at your age."

"I'm not that old," she said in her own defense.

"With the way you acted, I thought you had been raised by very strict parents who kept you sheltered from the outside world."

"You should have seen me the first time I experienced the bathroom," Andrea said, smiling.

Adam got up and began pacing back and forth. "Do you realize you could very well be the first person to actually travel through time and possibly stay for this length of time?" he asked.

"I thought you said you believed me?" Andrea whispered.

"I do," he said, "It's just hard to wrap my mind around, that's all."

"And you say my speech is strange," she mumbled.

Adam stopped and stared at her as a thought struck him. "Is there a possibility that you could go back?" he asked quietly.

"I don't know," she replied. "Sara and I discussed it, but couldn't figure out how it would be possible."

"I had a feeling Sara was in on this," he said. "I suppose that's why she was asking me all those questions about our family history."

"Sara was the only one I could trust."

"You could have trusted me," he said quietly.

Andrea shook her head. "I told you I was scared."

"How did you convince Sara you were telling the truth?"

"It was the pictures in your attic."

"Pictures in my attic?" Adam asked.

"There's a picture, a small tintype, of me in a box you have stored up there."

"Why would I have a picture of you in my attic?" he asked, frowning.

"This used to be my house, Adam," she replied.

"That's not possible," he stated. "This house has been in my family for generations. My great grandfather built it for his wife."

"Your great grandfather stole this house from my father," she said angrily. "He took advantage of my father's grief and talked him into turning this house over to him."

"Are you sure about that?"

"Yes, I'm sure," she replied. "One of those newspaper articles says that my father sold Nathan this house, but I still believe he stole it."

Adam looked at the article, and then shook his head. "You were actually engaged to my great grandfather," he said.

"No, I was never engaged to Nathan," she replied. "He had it in his head that I was going to be his wife and that's why he gambled with my father when he was drinking. Nathan knew my father would lose."

"Did you know my great grandmother?" he asked.

Andrea smiled. "Saralyn and I were best friends." A pained expression crossed her features. "I hate the thought of her and my father grieving, not knowing what happened to me."

He picked up the paper again and slapped it with his hand. "Well, she obviously got over her grief since she did marry Nathan and their marriage lasted quite a long time."

"I'm glad Saralyn found happiness, but that doesn't excuse Nathan for what he did to my father."

He stood and raised her chin to meet his gaze. "Does it matter now?" he asked quietly. "You're here, in this house." He kissed her tenderly as he wrapped his arms around her.

"Sara said the same thing," she whispered.

Adam pulled back as a thought struck him. "That's why you were so frightened of Nate. Because he resembles Nathan," he said quietly.

She nodded her head. "The first time I saw him, I thought I had seen a ghost."

"But you're not frightened of him anymore?"

"Not anymore," she replied. She hesitated a moment, then said, "Adam, Nate knows the whole story."

Adam frowned. "Why didn't he tell me?"

"I asked him not to. I told him I wanted to be the one to tell you," she replied. "He also warned me about Carol," she added.

"Carol? Does she know about this?"

"Not according to Nate," she replied. "But he said she was continuing her investigation of me and for me to watch my back. Whatever that means."

Adam sighed. "It means that Carol wants me and will do anything to make me see that you don't belong here."

"Do I?" she asked quietly.

"Yes, you do!" he whispered harshly. "If you were to leave me now, I don't know what I would do."

"What are you saying?"

"I'm saying that I love you, Andrea," he replied softly.

"You do? Really?" she whispered.

"I do, really," he replied, smiling.

"I have loved you from the first moment I saw you," she whispered, tears running down her cheeks.

"I could tell," he said, smiling.

"How could you tell?"

"By the way you made love with me," he whispered. "The look in your eyes when we made love spoke volumes."

His desire was manifested in a low moan as he cupped her chin in his hand and tilted her head back to receive his kiss. Passion sparked, ignited. Burned: hotter than ever.

He moved her backwards until they reached the bed. He removed her clothes and they pooled around her feet. Within moments, his followed the same path. He laid her down and his hands began a slow path down her body as his lips met hers.

Andrea moaned softly as heat rushed to every spot his hands touched.

He ran his hand softly over her abdomen and he gazed at her. "We never got around to talking about this," he said. "Are you sure you're pregnant?"

Andrea smiled. "I believe I am." And she was. With every fiber of her being, she knew she carried Adam's child.

"Then I guess I will have to make an honest woman out of you," he said.

"Are you asking me to marry you?" she whispered.

"Yes."

"Are you sure?"

"Very sure," he replied.

"What about my being from the past? How will you explain it to your friends?"

"Your past is no one's business but our own."

"Then, yes, I will marry you." She brought his head down and kissed him with all the love she felt within her heart.

They spent the entire day discussing the possibilities of how she had traveled through time. She told him about her father and how she had ended up in the woods the night she disappeared in her time.

That night, after Sara and Daniel had gone to bed, Adam and Andrea had returned to her room. Throughout the night, they had alternated between talking and making love.

Chapter 15

*A*dam had awakened just as the sun was beginning to rise and had gazed down at the woman lying beside him.   So much had happened last night. Andrea's amazing story of how she traveled through time had been totally amazing.

In the middle of the night, after making love several times, they had tiptoed up to the attic. Andrea had wanted to show Adam the pictures she and Sara had found.

She had shown him the boxes the pictures were in and pulling them from the shelf, had found the pictures of Nathan and her. The picture of her was faded and yellowed around the corners, but there was no mistaking it was her.

"Come on," he said, taking her hand. "There's a safe in the study that my father kept all his important papers in," he had told her. Taking the picture of Andrea with him, they had gone downstairs and he unlocked the safe. They went through several real estate documents until they located the ones he was looking for.

The first one was a deed from Jonathan Marsh to the National Bank of Chatham County dated December 1, 1861. It described the property and the amount of the loan from the bank to construct a house on the property. The second one was a deed from

Jonathan Marsh granting the property to Nathan Rivers.

There was another document in the package that Adam had never seen before. Pulling it out, he opened it and stared at it in surprise. It was the Will of Jonathan Marsh dated September 30, 1885. The sole heir to his fortune, including Briarcliff, was Andrea Marsh.

He'd handed the document to Andrea and watched as tears coursed down her cheeks as she read what was written on it. "These documents prove that this house *did* belong to me," she had said quietly.

"Yes, they do," he had told her.

She had looked up at him and smiled. "But you were right. It doesn't matter now because I am here, with you," she had said.

He'd placed the documents back in the safe and locked it, placing the picture back on the wall.

They had returned to her room and talked for a while. Adam had held her in his arms until she had drifted off to sleep.

He kissed her lightly and got out of bed and dressed as quietly as he could so he wouldn't wake her.

He went to his own room and removing his clothes for the second time that night and crawled in bed. He was asleep as soon as his head hit the pillow.

***

He woke to laughter outside his bedroom window. Pulling back the covers, he walked over to the window and laughed softly when he looked out and saw Andrea, Sara and Daniel playing a game of baseball. His smile turned to horror when he saw Andrea running around the makeshift bases and stumbled and fell.

He hurriedly pulled on his pants and grabbed his shirt, slipping his arms in the sleeves as he ran from the room. He took the stairs two at a time and ran out the front door.

Nate was in the library when he saw Adam fly through the foyer and out the door. Curious, he followed his brother.

"Are you all right?" Adam asked Andrea as he knelt down beside her.

"I'm fine," she replied, laughing. "Daniel told me I was supposed to slide to keep from being thrown out."

"Do you think you should be doing this? I mean, in your condition?" he asked worriedly.

"Adam, I'm okay," she assured him. She smiled shyly up at him and touched his lips with her fingertip. "As a matter of fact, I've never felt better," she whispered softly.

Adam growled low in his throat as he helped her up. "I just wish you'd be a little more careful," he said. He turned to Sara and Daniel. "Why don't you two go wash up for breakfast."

Daniel mumbled, but did as he was told. Sara beamed when she saw the look that passed between her father and Andrea. Everything was going to be all right, she told herself, as she followed Daniel to the house.

Nate had stood on the front porch, silently watching the exchange between his brother and Andrea. There was more going on than just mutual attraction. "Need some help over there, big brother?" he called out.

Adam frowned as he looked at Nate. "Everything's fine. We'll be there in a minute."

Nate hid a smile as he turned and went back in the house.

"I wish you wouldn't do things like this," Adam said, concern evident in his voice.

"I would never do anything to endanger this baby," she said quietly, placing a hand over her abdomen.

"Just promise me you'll be careful."

"I promise." She slid her fingers in between his and they walked back to the house.

When everyone had finished eating breakfast, Adam asked if they would stay, that he had something he wanted to tell them.

He reached over and took Andrea's hand and smiled at her. "Andrea and I are going to get married," he announced quietly.

Sara squealed with delight as she got up and hugged Andrea. "Is this what you really want?" she whispered in Andrea's ear.

"It's what I really want," Andrea assured her.

"Why you wanna go and do that for?" Daniel asked.

"Because we love each other," Adam replied.

"Yuck!" he said, making a face. "May I be excused?" he asked.

Adam laughed. "Yes, you may."

"Congratulations," Nate said quietly. "I hope you two will be very happy."

"Thank you," Andrea said. "If you will excuse me, I have some things I need to take care of before going out to the stables."

"You're going to work now?" Adam asked, frowning.

"It's my job, Adam," she responded quietly and left the two men sitting at the table.

"I think we need to talk," Nate said.

Here it comes, Adam thought. "If you're going to say I'm making a mistake, I don't want to hear it," he said.

"That's not what I was going to say," Nate said. "Believe it or not, I'm happy for you. I don't think I've ever seen you like this."

"I am happy," Adam said quietly as he poured himself another cup of coffee. "Andrea told me everything last night," he said, glancing sideways at his brother.

"Good," Nate breathed. "I take it she told you I already knew."

"Yes, she told me."

"You did believe her story, didn't you?" Nate asked.

"I had already suspected," he admitted. "And when I started putting all the pieces together, I had no choice."

"I can't imagine what it would feel like to wake up in a strange world in another time. This has got to be the most amazing thing that's ever happened."

"No one else can know about this, Nate." Adam said quietly. "If the government ever found out, she would be put in some military compound and put under a microscope. I would never see her or my baby again."

"Andrea's pregnant?" Nate gasped, surprised.

"We haven't announced that yet. We wanted to wait until after we're married. What's wrong?" he asked noticing the expression on Nate's face.

"This isn't good," Nate said.

"It's really none of your business," Adam said, anger tinting his voice.

"No, no, that's not what I mean," Nate said, shaking his head.

"Then what do you mean?"

"Carol."

"I really don't want to discuss her right now," Adam said frowning.

"I really think we need to," Nate insisted.

Adam sighed. "All right. What about her?"

"When she finds out about your impending marriage and that Andrea is pregnant, she's going to go ballistic."

"I don't owe her any explanation for what I do with my life," Adam said coldly.

"Have you seen her lately?" Nate asked.

"Not since she brought me those newspaper articles about Andrea."

"Well I've seen her and I think she's headed for the deep end. She's bound and determined to prove Andrea is a fraud and see that she's chased out of town."

"Right now she's just put out because I won't listen to her ranting. She'll come around eventually."

"Are you mad!?" Nate grated harshly. "The woman is fixated on you and she intends to have you, one way or the other."

"I think you're over-reacting, Nate," Adam stated flatly. "Carol and I are just friends."

Nate shook his head in disgust. "She's in love with you Adam, and right now, Andrea is an obstacle in her path. I guarantee you she will do anything to remove that obstacle to make sure you belong to her."

Adam stared at him in stunned surprise.

"Look, all I'm trying to say is that you need to be careful and you need to make sure Andrea is protected."

"I don't think Carol is capable of harming anyone," Adam said. "We've been friends too long and she would never do anything to hurt me."

"There's more you don't know, Adam."

"Excuse me," Catherine interrupted. "Adam, you have a phone call and the man says it's urgent he speak with you."

"Thank you, Catherine," he replied. He turned to Nate. "Don't worry about Carol."

Nate sighed as he shook his head again. He pushed away from the table and looked hard at his brother. "Don't say I didn't warn you," he said softly, leaving his brother to take his telephone call.

He went into the library and picked up the second line on the telephone and dialed Carol's number. She answered on the first ring. "I'm on my way over, stay put." If Adam wasn't going to do anything to stop Carol, he damn sure would.

Chapter 16

*C*arol was still in her nightgown when Nate arrived at her apartment. The long silk robe was open in the front exposing a generous amount of her breasts. Nate ignored her blatant display as he strode into the living room.

"What brings you here at this hour of the morning?" she asked.

"I just wanted to know how you were coming with your plans to get rid of Andrea," he said as he sat down on the sofa.

"What makes you think I have made any plans yet?" Carol asked in mock surprise.

Nate laughed softly. "I know you sweetheart," he replied. "After your botched attempt to get Adam to throw her out of his house, I know that pretty little head of yours is cooking something else up."

"And if I am?" she asked.

Nate shrugged. "Maybe I want to help," he replied.

Carol's eyes narrowed as she looked at him. "Why?"

"Because I know how much you love Adam and I'm sick of his holier than thou attitude," he replied. God, he hoped his face didn't betray what he was really feeling, he thought to himself.

Carol was silent for a moment, unsure whether she could trust him or not. She knew he and Adam didn't get along, but would he wage a full scale war against his own brother to help her?

As if he knew what she was thinking, Nate said, "Look, Adam and I aren't exactly on good terms anymore, but I still don't want him to get hurt. As long as whatever you're planning doesn't involve him, then I want to help you. This Andrea person should be exposed for what she is and be thrown in jail."

Carol sighed as she sat down across from him. "I haven't been able to find out any more on her," she said, conceding that he would help her.

"Why don't you call the police and expose her as a fraud?" Nate asked.

"Because Adam would make up some story to save her ass and then he would never speak to me again," she replied irritably.

"Then you must have some kind of a plan to get rid of her," Nate said, watching her closely.

She cut her eyes at him, and then smiled. "Nothing solid yet."

"Then tell me what you've got so far." He wanted her to tell him about Mike Stanton.

"I'd rather not say until I have all the details worked out," she responded.

"Come on, Carol. Maybe I can help work out those details for you," he urged.

She shook her head. "No, I'll tell you when I have everything ready to set into motion."

Nate clenched his jaw, wanting desperately to wipe that smirk off her face. "How long?" he asked instead.

She shrugged. "A day; maybe two."

He got up and walked to the door. "You'll let me know?"

"Just as soon as I have everything set," she replied.

He nodded and closed the door behind him. He wanted to go back in there and put his hands around her throat and shake the truth out of her. But, he didn't. Instead, he got into his car and sped away from the curb.

"You'll know what I've got planned for Andrea Marsh at the same time your brother does," Carol whispered to the empty room. Humming to herself, she went into her bedroom and began changing her clothes.

The day after tomorrow would be a glorious day for her. She would finally be rid of Andrea Marsh and if Adam showed any signs of grief, well she would be there for him just as she had been there for him when Amanda had fallen to her death.

She picked up the telephone and dialed Stanton's number. When he answered, she told him what she wanted him to do and when.

"I told you I won't do that. If you want her dead, then you'll have to do it yourself. I want no part of it," he stated coldly.

"You said you wanted your revenge on Adam," she reminded him.

He laughed harshly. "I think I already have it."

"What do you mean? What did you do?"

"Him having to deal with you is revenge enough for me."

"Bastard!" she growled as she slammed the telephone down.

I don't need him, she said to herself. "I can take care of Andrea Marsh without anyone's help," she whispered. "And I know just how to do it."

***

Sara pestered Adam and Andrea all evening to set a wedding date. The three of them were sitting in the living room after Daniel had gone to bed. Her excitement over the upcoming events had her babbling all night.

Daniel had even gotten in on the discussion earlier and had become excited that he would soon have a new mommy.

Sara looked at Andrea as if she had lost her mind when she said that a June wedding would be lovely. "You can't wait that long! You'll be showing by then," she cried.

Adam and Andrea had spoken to Sara and told her that he knew everything. Sara had been so relieved and happy that her father believed them. She had apologized to Adam for keeping the secret, but explained that she couldn't betray Andrea. He had told her that he understood and that everything would be all right.

Andrea frowned as she looked at Adam. "Would that be an embarrassment for you?" she asked quietly.

Adam smiled and shook his head. "No, but it would be for you," he replied.

"What do you mean?"

"What he means is that everyone in this town doesn't need to know that you two did it before you got married," Sara answered in Adam's place.

Andrea's face turned red at her implication and Adam scowled at his daughter.

"I'm not ashamed of what your father and I did," Andrea told her.

"Does anybody care what I think?" Adam asked angrily. Both of them looked at him at the tone of his voice.

"Sorry," Sara said meekly.

"Me too," Andrea said.

"To save both of you from any embarrassment and to make me happy, I think we should get married tomorrow."

"What?!" Andrea gasped.

"Why not?" Adam returned.

"I have nothing to wear to be married in," she argued.

"Yea," Sara jumped in. "we have to get her a wedding dress and Mrs. Floyd has to bake the cake and make all the preparations and…"

"All right, all right," Adam said, holding up a hand. "I was only kidding."

Andrea breathed a sigh of relief. "What about the fifteenth of next month?" Andrea asked. "That's the day I was born and I think it would be nice to get married on that day."

"Really? And just how old will you be?" Adam asked, teasingly.

"Twenty-five," she replied softly.

"Then the fifteenth of next month it is," he said, then looked at Sara. "Does that meet with your approval?"

Sara grinned and nodded her head. "Can I be your Maid of Honor?" she asked Andrea.

"I would be honored," Andrea told her.

"Is Uncle Nate going to be your Best Man?" Sara asked her father.

"I hope so," Adam replied.

"By the way, where is he?" Sara asked. "I haven't seen him since this morning at breakfast."

"I don't know where he went, but I'm sure he'll be happy to be my Best Man," Adam said. "Now, it's time for you to go to bed," he told Sara.

She kissed Adam on the cheek and hugged Andrea.

When she was out of the room, Andrea turned to Adam. "What did you and Nate talk about after I left this morning?"

He pulled her into his arms and kissed her. "Nothing for you to worry about," he replied.

"It was about me, wasn't it?" she asked, looking at him.

He sighed as he leaned his head against the back of the sofa. "It seems my brother is concerned for your safety," he said.

"Why would he be con...oh, Carol," she said, a frown creasing her brow. "I don't understand why she hates me so much."

"Because you have what she wants," he told her.

"I do?" she asked in mock surprise.

Adam pulled her tighter against him. "You have something that she never will. You have my heart," he whispered.

"Oh, Adam," she whispered as she met his lips.

***

Andrea had never been so exhausted. She and Sara had spent hours shopping for her wedding dress the following weekend and she had finally settled on a simple white dress, telling Sara that she didn't want or need anything fancy. They were going to be married at home with only the family present and Mrs. Floyd.

When they got home later that afternoon, she went upstairs and took a hot shower and changed her clothes. Deciding to rest before dinner, she lay down on the bed and closed her eyes.

A tear slid down her cheek as the image of her father's face flashed in her mind. "I miss you, daddy. I wish you were here to see me get married and to give birth to your grandchild," she whispered.

She loved Adam deeply and was very happy, but she couldn't help missing her father. She prayed that somehow he knew how happy she was and that she had finally found love.

***

"Where have you been?" Adam asked Nate when he found him in his study, pacing back and forth.

"Out," he replied curtly.

"Out where? I've been looking everywhere for you. There's something I wanted to talk to you about."

Nate stopped pacing. Maybe Adam was ready to discuss what they were going to do about Carol.

"I want you to be my Best Man," Adam said.

"What?" Nate said, confusion written on his face.

"I said, I want you to be my Best Man," Adam repeated.

"I was hoping you were finally going to listen to me about Carol," Nate said, frowning.

Adam sighed. "Her again?"

"Damn it, Adam!" Nate growled. "She's up to something and I tell you it isn't good!"

"How do you know she's up to something?"

"Why do you think I showed up here so suddenly?" Nate asked him. At Adam's frown, he continued. "Carol called me and told me she needed my help. She sounded pretty upset and since we've been friends for such a long time, I agreed. She said she wanted Andrea out of her way, Adam."

"And you agreed to help her?" Adam asked, his voice dangerously low.

"At first, yes." he replied angrily. "I was still angry over what happened the last time I was here."

"So what made you change your mind?"

"I guess I owned up to my responsibilities. I left after father died, angry that he left you everything, and when I returned, I swore revenge on you."

"That's when you decided to go after my wife," Adam said coldly.

"Yes. In the beginning, I went after Amanda to get back at you. But then we fell in love with each other. But you refused to give her a divorce."

"For Sara's and Daniel's sake," Adam said quietly. "After our argument that night, I realized that it did no good to hang onto someone that didn't want me, so I was going to give her the divorce. But it was too late."

"I didn't know that, so I blamed you for her death."

"So when Carol asked you to help her, you agreed."

I didn't agree to help her do anything," Nate replied angrily. "I only *pretended* to agree so I could find out what she was up to."

"And?"

"And nothing!" Nate replied savagely. "She accused me of falling for Andrea's lies like you have. But, I know she's planning something Adam, I just don't know what it is yet."

"Nate, this is Carol we're talking about," Adam said. "She's been our friend, *my friend*, for a long time. I just don't believe she's this evil person you keep saying she is."

"How do you think Amanda went over that cliff?" Nate asked quietly.

The blood drained from Adam's face. "She was thrown from her horse. It was an accident," he whispered.

Nate shook his head violently. "Carol pushed her off that cliff, Adam."

"How do you know this?"

"I just know."

"Why would Carol want to kill Amanda?" Adam asked, narrowing his eyes.

Nate shifted uncomfortably and looked around the room, avoiding his brother's eyes. Frowning suddenly, he asked, "Where's Andrea?"

"She's upstairs," Adam replied shortly. "Answer my question."

"Are you sure?" Nate insisted.

Adam jumped up and headed for the door. He stopped and turned to Nate. "This discussion is not over." he growled.

He took the stairs two at a time and burst through Andrea's bedroom door. He sighed with relief when he saw that she was sound asleep. He crawled in beside her and gathered her in his arms.

She opened her eyes and smiled. "Hi," she whispered sleepily.

"Hi," he whispered back.

She saw the worried look on his face. "Is anything wrong?" she asked.

"Not anymore," he replied. "Did you find a wedding dress?" he asked.

"Um," she replied, closing her eyes as she snuggled against him.

"I love you," he whispered, Andrea didn't respond. She had already gone back to sleep.

He sighed heavily and went back over his conversation with his brother. Why was Nate saying these things about Carol? Did he truly believe that Carol would actually do harm to Andrea? And did he truly believe that she had killed Amanda?

Adam couldn't believe such a thing about Carol. He had known her a long time and she had been his friend through the rough times in his life.

He pulled Andrea closer against his body and closed his eyes. He was happier than he had been in years and nothing or no one was going to take that away.

Chapter 17

*S*he felt the sun beat down on her as she rode through the woods and smiled. She was happy. She was going to have Adam's child and they were going to be married next month.

As she rode, her thoughts went to the previous night when she had woken up in Adam's arms. They had made love and she had fallen back to sleep. When she woke up this morning, the pillow beside her was empty. He still insisted that he not be found in her room because he didn't want her to be embarrassed.

So engrossed in her thoughts, she didn't notice another rider until the horse was a few feet in front of her. She frowned when she saw Carol sliding down from her horse and Andrea did the same.

"What are you doing here?" Andrea asked.

"You're not going to get away with it," Carol said coldly.

"I don't know what you're talking about," Andrea said.

"You show up here using a dead woman's name and throw yourself at Adam."

"That's not true!" Andrea gasped.

"Hell, you've even got Nate believing your lies as well," she went on, ignoring Andrea's cry. "Adam is mine," she spat. "Do you think I went to all that trouble of getting rid of Amanda so another woman could have him?"

"What did you do to Amanda?" Andrea gasped, horrified.

"It was an accident," Carol replied, shrugging. "I didn't realize how close to the edge of the cliff we were. She stumbled and fell backwards." She looked around and an ugly smiled appeared on her face. "As a matter of fact, it happened right over there," she pointed behind where Andrea was standing.

"She was so self righteous, calling me a whore. She was the whore." Her gaze was fixed on a point beyond Andrea as she continued. "She had the most wonderful man in love with her, but it wasn't enough. She had to have his brother as well. When Adam found out about them, I thought for sure he would make her leave."

"Adam told me he was going to give her a divorce." Andrea whispered.

"What?"

"It's true," she said.

"That's a lie," Carol said. "Adam told me he would never let her go."

"No, Adam told me that he had finally agreed to give Amanda her divorce," Andrea said.

"It doesn't matter," she growled. "Even if they had divorced, she would still have been around, bothering us." She focused her gaze on Andrea. "Now, you're in the way and I can't have that."

"I won't be in your way, Carol. I'll leave today," Andrea said.

Carol's eyes narrowed. "You're lying," she accused.

"No, I promise, I'll leave today." She took a step to go around her, but Carol grabbed her arm.

"I can't take that chance." Andrea began to struggle as Carol began pulling her toward the edge of the cliff.

"Carol, don't do this," she begged.

"I have to!" she screamed, pulling harder. Her eyes became wild as she dragged Andrea by the arm.

"Carol, please, don't hurt my baby!" Andrea whispered pleadingly.

Carol stopped dead in her tracks and a look of total outrage covered her face. Too late Andrea realized her mistake.

She pushed hard against her chest and Andrea stumbled backwards. She screamed as she felt herself falling. Terrified and unable to grab onto anything, she cried out Adam's name.

Carol smirked when she heard the pitiful cry. Leaning over the edge, she grinned as she looked at the twisted remains of Andrea's body lying on the ledge below.

***

Nate had watched Andrea ride off on Max from the living room window. When she hadn't returned within a couple of hours, he began to worry.

Carol had refused to include him in on her plans and he was afraid she and Stanton had gone ahead with them. He had been unable to track Stanton down after he had left Rodie's that night. He wasn't registered at any of the motels or hotels in or around town. But that didn't mean he wasn't still in contact with Carol.

He glanced at the clock once again and headed for the front door. Going out to the stables, he quickly saddled a horse and rode off in the direction Andrea had taken earlier.

As he came out on the other side of the woods, an uneasy feeling took hold of him. He slid off his horse and tied him to a tree and walked around the area, calling her name. Receiving no response, he started to climb back on his horse when something hanging on a tree branch caught his eye. He walked over to it and before even touching it, knew it belonged to Andrea.

A moaned escaped his lips as he hesitantly peered over the edge, sure he would find Andrea's body lying at the bottom.

Releasing the breath he didn't realize he had been holding, he backed up. He heard a noise behind him and turned suddenly. Max was standing there eyeing him solemnly.

"Okay, boy, where's Andrea?" he asked the horse as he walked up to him. He called out her name and again and still got no response.

He ran the scarf in his hand against his face and could still smell her fragrance. He remembered seeing it tied around her waist when she left the house that morning. So how did it get from her waist and stuck on a tree branch? Had someone else been here with her? He wondered silently.

"Carol!" he growled as understanding came to him. He jumped on his horse and, grabbing Max's reins, went back to the house.

To his utter surprise, he saw Carol walking up the front steps that led to the house. Pulling on the reins, he slowed his horse down and jumped off.

He grabbed Carol's arm and spun her around. "Where is she?" he demanded angrily.

"Where's who?" Carol returned, surprised.

"You know who!" he snapped. "What the hell have you done with her?"

"Nate, darling, I do believe you've been out in the sun too long," she said sweetly.

"Where the hell is Andrea?"

"Why would I know where she is?" she returned.

"Because you know Adam is in love with her and that you've lost," he replied coldly.

"That's a lie!" she snapped. "Adam would never love someone like her. He loves me."

"Dear God! Would you listen to yourself?" he laughed harshly. "Adam has never loved you and never will. He's going to marry Andrea and there's nothing you can do to stop him."

"We'll see," she said smugly.

"You're right, we will," he said, grabbing her arm and dragging her into the house.

"What the hell!" Adam said when he heard the commotion in the foyer. He watched stunned as his brother dragged Carol into the living room.

"Let me go!" Carol cried as she continued to struggle for release.

"Nate, you want to tell me what the hell is going on?" Adam demanded.

Nate yelled when he felt Carol's teeth sink into his arm. "You bitch!" he growled as he drew back his hand.

"Nate!" Adam yelled. "Let her go!"

Nate lowered his hand but did not release her. "If I let her go, she'll run," he told Adam.

"You still haven't told me why you dragged her in here," Adam reminded him.

Carol tried to pull away again, but he only tightened his grip. "Andrea is missing and Carol had something to do with it."

Adam stiffened. "How do you know she's missing?"

"When she didn't come back from her ride this morning, I went looking for her," he replied, taking the scarf from his pocket and handing it to Adam. "I found this caught on a tree branch near the edge of the cliff."

No one saw the look in Carol's eyes when she saw the scarf. She tried frantically pulling out of Nate's grasp again.

The blood drained from Adam's face as he took the scarf. He looked at Nate as he fought to keep his hold on Carol. "You think she had something to do with Andrea's disappearance?"

"I tried to tell you what she's capable of, but you wouldn't listen," Nate ground out.

Adam glanced at Carol then back at his brother. "Do you have any proof that she has done any harm to Andrea?" he asked quietly.

"Well, no, but—"

"Then, let her go."

"Adam!"

"Let her go!" Adam snapped. "Without proof, there's not a damned thing we can do," he added.

Nate released her so hard, she fell against the sofa. Rubbing her arm, she glared at Nate.

"Let's go," Adam told Nate. He bent down close to Carol and whispered softly, "If I find out that you had anything to do with this, I'll kill you with my bare hands."

Nate glared at her as he followed his brother.

***

Every muscle in her body ached and it was all she could do to remain still as the deafening roar overwhelmed her. She could barely breathe and didn't know if she could move as pain assaulted her from every direction.

She opened her eyes and blinked furiously several times to clear her vision. She breathed a small sigh of relief as she looked around her at the familiar landscape. Slowly, sending signals to each muscle in her body, she tried to move. Sharp pain shot through her head and she gasped as she fell back into unconsciousness.

"Open your eyes. Ms. Marsh! Wake up!"

She wanted to wake up; she wanted to make the pain stop.

"Can you open your eyes?"

She blinked and then abruptly closed them again. "Adam…?"

"You're going to be all right," a man's voice said to her.

She forced her eyes open and stared at the stranger. Confused, she could only mutter, "What…?"

"We've been looking for you for several days," the man said. "Your daddy is sure gonna be happy."

"Where am I? What happened? Where's… where's Adam?"

"Ain't no Adam here, Ms. Marsh."

She looked closer at her surroundings and then she remembered the last time she had been here and fear raced through her body. She closed her eyes and thought of Adam and his gentle touch when he made love to her. She tried to think of Sara, of the beautiful young girl with the stunning smile. And Daniel, with his grown up ways and mischievous smile.

"I need Adam," she whispered. Looking at the other men surrounding her, she gasped at their clothing. "No…" she moaned softly. "I can't be here. I have to…"

She couldn't finish her words as the pain seemed to wrap around her head. This couldn't be happening. It couldn't. It couldn't…

Chapter 18

Her forehead was cold. Her eyelids barely opened and she squinted at the sun coming through the open window. Andrea couldn't figure out at first where she was, or how she got into this bed. Her head ached, as if a steel band were tightening around it. Raising her fingers to her face, she felt a cold compress had been placed on her forehead.

She slowly opened her eyes and stared at the man sitting beside the bed.

"Where am I?"

He smiled and his slightly worn features were creased with a frown. "You're going to be all right now."

At the sound of her father's voice, she felt tears at the back of her eyes.

"Honey, please…can you tell me what happened to you?" her father pleaded, clutching Andrea's right hand.

"I…I'm not sure," Andrea muttered through the tightness in her throat. What could she say? Her brain was still trying to make sense of what had happened. She wondered if she were dreaming and would wake up in Adam's arms…or was he a dream?

Jonathan stared at her with a worried expression. There were so many questions he wanted to ask her. For instance, where did she get the clothes she was wearing? When she ran from the house a week ago, she was wearing her emerald gown. Had someone found her and given her the men's clothing? And, if someone had found her, why didn't they bring her home? Had she been kidnapped and had somehow gotten away?

"Doc Phelps says you're going to be all right. Can you remember anything?"

She could only nod. "Yes…something happened."

Jonathan reached out and touched her forehead and placed a kiss upon her cheek. It felt warm and loving and Andrea found herself smiling at the familiarity.

"They're calling it a miracle, you know. We've been searching for you for a week, and then all of a sudden, you're there."

Andrea could only stare blankly at her father. A week? How could that be possible? She had spent over three months with Adam! She remembered him, Sara, and Daniel; all of them. They were *real*. It had been every bit as real as this room and her father's kiss. Somehow, in the space of moments, timeless moments, she had been taught to live in the future, and to escape *time*!

Panic was right at the edge of her consciousness and she breathed deeply. Adam *was* real. To deny the love she had experienced with him would be insane. She ran her hand over her abdomen as a tear slipped from her eye. This was real; Adam's child growing within her!

"Andrea, are you all right? Are you in pain?" her father asked worriedly.

She shook her head as she wiped the tears from her eyes.

"No one thought to search the cliff area."

"What?" she whispered.

"I said, no one thought to search the cliff area, it being so far from the house," he repeated. "How in the world did you get there?"

Suddenly, it all came back to her. She had gone for a ride on Max and when she came to the clearing beyond the woods, Carol had been there. She had been crazed and had pushed her off the edge of the cliff.

Did Adam know? Was he searching for her this very minute? Had her body disappeared as it had the first time?

"I'm sorry for everything that happened between us," Jonathan was saying.

She focused on him again and took his hand. "It doesn't matter," she spoke softly. She tried to get up and a wave of dizziness assaulted her.

"Lie still," Jonathan cautioned gently. "You banged your head pretty hard. Doc says you're going to be sore for a few days."

She gingerly touched the knot on her forehead and grimaced. "I have to go back," she whispered.

"Go back? Go back where?"

"I have to get back to Adam," she whispered, trying to sit up again.

"Andrea, you're confused. There is no one named Adam here."

"Father, you don't understand. Adam will be searching for me and will worry if he cannot find me."

Jonathan frowned deeply. She must have hit her head really hard, he thought. "Let me get the doctor and have him take another look at you," he suggested.

"I don't need a doctor," she snapped. At the hurt in his eyes, she apologized. "I'm sorry. There's just so much you don't understand."

"We'll have plenty of time to talk later. Right now, you need your rest." He kissed her forehead.

She watched him leave the room and then closed her eyes. "Oh, Adam, come find me, please…"

***

"Is she awake yet?" Nathan asked when Jonathan closed the door to her room. He had been pacing back and forth in front of her door since she was brought in.

The entire staff had been whispering all morning about Andrea's miraculous return. Nathan still had his doubts. Where had she been for the past week? And why had she been wearing men's clothes when they found her?

One of her shoes had been found near the lake the night of her disappearance, so how did she end up beyond the woods? And how did she get to the bottom of the cliff? Had she been walking too close to the edge and fallen?

"I want to talk to her," he told Jonathan as he started to open the door.

"Nathan, wait," Jonathan said, halting him. "I think Doc Phelps needs to take another look at her."

"Why? What's wrong?"

"She's acting strange, really confused about where she is and who everyone is," he replied. He didn't want to tell Nathan that she was asking for someone by the name of Adam. Until he could find out more about this Adam man, he would keep this to himself.

"Of course she's a little confused. She's got a pretty nasty bump on her head," Nathan said.

"What she needs right now is rest. There will be plenty of time later to find out what happened."

"Did she tell you *anything*?" Nathan asked, frowning.

He shook his head. "I don't think she remembers too much right now," he replied. "But, I'm sure that

208

when she's had some rest, she will be able to tell us something."

Nathan felt Jonathan was keeping something from him, but decided to let it go for now. He agreed and the two of them went into the parlor.

***

As soon as the door closed, Andrea pulled back the covers and slowly sat up. She felt another wave of dizziness and grabbed hold of the bedpost to steady herself. She glanced around the room at all the familiar things. Her toiletries were still on her vanity, along with the paintings of her, her mother and father. Everything was as she had left it.

A quick knock came at the door and before Andrea could answer, Mattie entered with a huge smile and tears in her eyes.

"I was so worried about you," Mattie whispered, gathering Andrea into her arms. "First, they said you had run away, and then they said you was kidnapped."

"I wasn't kidnapped, Mattie," Andrea said, smiling at the woman who had cared for her since she was a small child.

"It don't matter, you're home now."

"Yes," Andrea whispered softly. "I'm home."

"I bet what you need right now is a good hot bath to ease some of them aches and pains," Mattie suggested.

No, what I need is a hot shower. Andrea thought to herself. She never thought she would miss the modern conveniences of a bathroom.

Mattie left and returned a short time later with Will and Joseph who placed a large round hammered-copper tub in the room. Two young girls Andrea had never seen before came in carrying pails of steaming water.

After everyone left, Andrea walked over to the tub and put her fingers into the water. It was hot and enticing and slipping out of her clothes, she crawled in and slowly sat down. She closed her eyes as the warmth began to ease her tired aching body.

She took a deep breath and exhaled slowly. Her mind wandered to the luxuries of modern conveniences and Adam's home, where they must be worried, searching for her.

What had happened to her...really? Carol had pushed her over the edge of the cliff and she remembered falling backward. That much she knew, and she remembered feeling like she'd been hurled into a relentless tempest of wind. She recalled the intense pain that had racked her body and the fleeting thought that she might be dying. Then she had hit her head and then, nothing.

Deciding it was time to get out of the water, she grabbed the length of cloth that hung from the handle of the tub and wrapped it around her body. A quick knock came at the door and Mattie entered carrying a tray of food.

Andrea smiled and thanked Mattie as she walked to the dresser and pulled out a white cotton gown and handed it to her. "Thank you," Andrea said softly.

"I tell you, everyone has been besides themselves since you disappeared," Mattie said. "Miss Saralyn didn't want to go home, but your daddy made her. Told her there was nothing she could do here seein's how she had a sick momma at home to take care of."

"Saralyn," Andrea whispered. She lightly touched her abdomen. The child she carried would be Saralyn's great, great grandchild. She frowned. "Her mother is sick?"

"Yes, Ms. Grace fell and broke her leg, so Miss Saralyn had to go home and take care of her."

"I'm sorry," Andrea said quietly.

"She sure was mad at your daddy and Mr. Nathan when you disappeared," she chuckled softly. "I do believe Miss Saralyn would have kilt Mr. Nathan had she had a gun on her."

No, she was not going to kill him, Andrea thought silently, because within a few short months, she would become his wife. If only she could get back to Adam.

"I'm sorry I caused so much trouble for everyone," Andrea said.

Mattie snorted. "Not that Mr. Nathan and Mr. Jonathan didn't deserve it, after what they done to you."

"You know what happened?"

"Ain't much I don't knows round here."

"I had no intention of marrying Nathan and never will," she told Mattie.

"I knows that," she replied, picking up the clothes Andrea had been wearing.

"You get something in your stomach and get back in bed," she ordered and left the room with them.

Andrea slipped the gown over her head and let out a sigh. Okay, this was it. She was here, for now. She would deal with everything tomorrow, when she'd had time to think. She glanced at the tray Mattie had left and felt the rumble in her stomach. Yes, she would deal with everything tomorrow.

Chapter 19

*S*he felt the sun's comforting warmth against her face as her eyelids fluttered open. Snuggling into the soft pillow, she sighed. She had been dreaming of Adam and how happy they had been.

A soft knock sounded at the door and Andrea's eyes flew open. Nathan stood in the doorway, smiling at her as he asked if he could come in.

Quickly, she slipped up to the headboard and clutched the covers to her chest.

"How are you feeling this morning?" he asked as he pulled up a stool next to the bed and sat down.

"Better," she replied.

"Have you been able to remember anything yet?"

"Where's father?" she asked.

"I believe he's still in bed," Nathan replied. "The past week has been really hard for him."

"I never meant to cause my father any worry," she said, frowning.

"I'm sure you didn't," he told her. "Can you tell me what happened? How you ended up where you were found; at the bottom of the cliff?"

Andrea sighed as she laid her head back. A tear slipped from the corner of her eye and she reached up to wipe it away. "The last thing I remember is running and then falling. I must have been too close to the edge of the cliff and went over. I don't remember anything until those men found me."

"Surely if you went over the cliff, you would not be here to tell about it," he said, watching her closely.

Her eyes rounded her horror. "You're right. By all accounts, I should be dead. But, maybe something broke my fall, you think?"

Nathan narrowed his eyes. "You have no idea how you got to the cliff? No idea why you were wearing men's clothing?"

"I was wearing men's clothing?!" she gasped.

"Yes."

She shook her head. "I don't know, Nathan. Could it be possible that someone found me and tried to help me?" she asked.

"Then why didn't they bring you home when they found out who you were?"

"I don't know. Maybe I ran away from them and somehow lost my way and ended up near the cliff." She rubbed her temples with the tips of her fingers. "Can we not talk about this now? I believe I'm beginning to get a headache."

"Very well," he told her as he stood. "But, we do have to have this discussion, and soon."

Andrea released a sigh as the door closed behind him. He was the last person she would tell her story to. But she did have to tell her father and she had to make him believe her and help her get back to Adam.

She pulled the covers back and crawled out of bed. Walking over to the wardrobe, she grimaced at all the fancy gowns still hanging there. She chose a simple one and not bothering to put on a corset, slipped it over her head. Running a brush quickly through her hair, she went in search of her father.

He wasn't in his room and when she didn't find him in the library, she went into the kitchen and asked Mattie where he was.

"Yor daddy had to go back to town to deliver the rest of them horses that he took over a couple of days ago. Said to tell you he would be back by dinner time."

Sighing softly to herself, she poured herself a cup of coffee and grimaced at the taste. She had forgotten just how strong Mattie made it; she was so used to the coffee Mrs. Floyd made.

"Do you happen to know where Nathan is?" she asked.

Mattie made a disgusting sound with her lips and said, "He left a while ago and by God's grace, he won't return."

Andrea smiled at her and Mattie began to prepare Andrea's breakfast when she told her all she wanted was some bread and coffee. Mattie argued, but did as she was told.

After she finished the small meal, she went into her father's study and sat down at his desk. Opening the top drawer, she began looking through his papers. When she found what she was looking for, she pulled it out and began to read it.

"This has to be put in a safe place," she told herself as she glanced around the room. Spotting the painting on the wall over the hearth, she walked over to it and took it down. She breathed a sigh of relief when she saw the small safe.

Going back over to the desk, she searched through all the drawers until she found a piece of paper with numbers written on it. Taking the paper back over to the safe, she turned the knob until she heard a click. Opening the safe, she gasped in shock when she saw the bundles of money stacked inside. What would her father be doing with so much money? She wondered. Why didn't he keep this amount of money in a bank?

Shaking her head, she placed the papers inside and closed it, turning the knob until it was locked.

She placed the piece of paper with the combination on it back in the desk drawer and smiling softly to herself, left her father's study.

When she walked into the library, sadness filled her. This was where she and Adam had spent several nights curled up on the sofa talking and planning their future.

Tears filled her eyes at the thought of never seeing him again. How could she go on without him? She touched her stomach and felt the slightest movement of her child. How would she explain to him or her, that his or her father lived in another world?

She had to get back. Somehow, she had to find a way to return to Adam and their future.

***

Andrea spent the rest of the day in her room, trying to figure out a way to get back to Adam. She hoped that when she told her father, he would believe her and possibly help her come up with a way to get back to the future.

When she went back downstairs late that afternoon, she found him in the library staring into the fire. "Father," she called his name softly.

"Andrea!" he said, surprised to see her up. "Should you be out of bed so soon?" he asked.

"I'm feeling better," she told him. "Father, we need to talk."

"Did Nathan speak with you?"

Andrea frowned. "He came to see me this morning," she replied. "Why?"

"What did he tell you?"

"He just wanted to know how I was feeling."

Jonathan sighed as he ran a hand through his hair. "Nathan still insists that you marry him," he said quietly.

"That's not going to happen," Andrea said.

"If you don't marry him by the end of the week, he's going to foreclose on the ranch."

"He's not going to do that, father."

"You don't know him, Andrea."

"I can't marry Nathan, ever."

"Why?"

"I'm carrying another man's child," she replied quietly.

"You don't have to make up excuses, Andrea. Nathan won't accept any of them."

"It's not an excuse." How was she going to explain this to him?

"Father, what I'm going to tell you will seem insane, but I promise you it's the truth. I can't tell you how or why it happened, but that week I was missing here, it was actually three months in the future." She saw the utter disbelief in his eyes, but continued. "The night I left the house, it started storming. When I tried to come back, I fell and hit my head and was knocked unconscious. When I woke up, I was over one hundred years into the future."

"Dear God!" Jonathan breathed as he got up and started for the door.

"Where are you going?" Andrea asked, puzzled.

"I'm going to have Mattie summons the doctor," he replied. "You were obviously hurt more seriously than we thought."

Andrea laughed softly. "I haven't lost my mind, father. What I'm telling you is the truth."

"It just isn't possible, Andrea."

"Come sit back down and let me finish telling you everything," she coaxed gently.

Jonathan hesitated a moment, then went and did as she asked. He stared at his daughter as she continued her amazing story.

"I didn't believe it myself, at first, but when I saw all the modern things like the kitchen, My God, you should have seen it! There were such things they called "appliances" in it. And the bathroom; there was water coming out of spouts in the walls. It was all so frightening. But I got used to it all and began to enjoy everything. I even got to take a shower. It's like standing beneath a waterfall, only there's hot and cold water coming from it."

Andrea laughed at the look of horror on her father's face. "It's all true. I don't know what I would have done without Sara to help me adjust."

"Who is Sara?" he asked, when he was able to form words.

"Sara is Adam's daughter."

"You asked for someone named Adam when they found you. Is this the man who got you with child?"

"Yes," she replied, smiling. "I love him very much and we are, were going to be married next month."

"Andrea, how is all this possible?"

"I'm not really sure," she replied, frowning slightly. "Adam told me it's called time travel, that there is a parallel world to this one and somehow, I was thrown into the future during the storm."

Jonathan was still having a hard time believing her story. "If the storm is what carried you to this other world, then what brought you back here? Was there another storm?"

"No, there was no storm. I think that when Carol pushed me off the cliff, I must have traveled back in time."

"Now, who is Carol?"

Andrea explained about Carol and how she had tried to get Adam to make her leave. "When I told Carol that I was carrying Adam's child, she became enraged and pushed me off the cliff."

Jonathan shook his head. "Andrea, I believe you had a terrible nightmare and you woke up thinking it was true."

She grabbed his hand and placed it on her abdomen. Tears forming in her eyes, she whispered, "Can you feel the life growing inside me? That's not a dream!"

He gasped in shock and jerked his hand away when he felt a slight movement beneath his hand.

"It's not a dream, father. It's real."

Jonathan had never felt so frightened before. The possibility of what she was saying was unbelievable. But he had felt the slightest movement beneath his hand and when he looked into his daughter's eyes, he knew she spoke the truth.

"What are you going to do?" he whispered.

"Oh, father!" she breathed, hugging him. "I knew you would believe me!"

"Your story is too crazy even for you to make up," he said, laughing nervously.

She grinned and kissed his cheek. "Now, you see why I cannot marry Nathan?"

"He's going to be very angry," Jonathan warned.

"If I marry Nathan now, it will change the future and Adam will never be born."

"He'll take the ranch."

"But you will live here until it is time for you to be with mother again," she told him gently.

"How do you know that?"

She told him about finding the newspaper articles and Nathan marrying Saralyn and how the Rivers' line would continue.

"How do you plan to get back?"

"I could knock myself unconscious and hope that when I wake up I will be with Adam again?" Sighing heavily, she shook her head. "I have no idea how I'm going to get back."

Chapter 20

*N*ate watched as Adam paced back and forth. "Maybe we should call the police," he suggested.

"And tell them what?" Adam asked.

"That Andrea is missing and we think we know what happened to her," he replied.

"The police will have to file a missing report and you know what they will find," he said. "I think we should just wait and see what happens before we bring them in."

"You're right. So what are we going to do?"

"We're going back and see if we might have missed something."

"Adam, we searched the whole damned area. She's not there," Nate said exasperated.

"We've got to try!" he yelled.

"Okay, okay," Nate sighed. "We'll go back and take another look."

"You still think Carol had something to do with Andrea's disappearance, don't you?"

"With every fiber in my body!" Nate replied harshly.

Suddenly, Adam stopped pacing and spun around, his eyes portraying the horror he was beginning to feel. "What if she went back?" he whispered.

"You mean back to the past?" Adam nodded and Nate continued. "How would she get back? There was a storm the night she arrived here, but not one when she disappeared."

Adam sighed heavily. "Let's just go and have another look," he said.

"I'm with you," Nate said.

The two men went out to the stables and saddled their horses and rode as fast as they could through the woods.

When they got to the other side, they tied their horses and started combing the area again.

"Son of a bitch!" Adam swore as he bent down and picked something up that was lying near the edge of the cliff.

"What is it?" Nate asked, joining him.

"Does this look familiar?"

"Now do you believe me?" Nate asked harshly, taking the diamond earring Adam held in his hand.

"I'm going to kill her," Adam said coldly.

"Not before I do," Nate growled.

They climbed back on their horses and headed back to the house. Handing the reins to one of the stable boys, the two men climbed into Adam's car and sped out of the driveway.

When they pulled up in front of Carol's apartment building, Nate stopped Adam before he opened his door.

"How are we going to handle this?" he asked.

"I'm going to go in there and wrap my hands around her throat and strangle the truth out of her," Adam replied angrily.

"She's not going to tell us anything if you frighten her."

"Then what do you suggest?"

"Let me go in and try to talk to her. If I handle it right, maybe she'll confess."

"Nate, she knows you suspect her. Why the hell would she confess to you?"

"You're right. Let's go strangle the truth out of her," he said coldly.

Adam knocked on her door and got no response. He knocked louder and told her to open up. She still didn't respond, so he yelled, "Carol, if you don't open this door, I'm going to break it down!"

"You don't have to be so violent, Adam," Carol said when she finally opened the door. She frowned slightly when she saw Nate standing behind him. "I was momentarily indisposed."

Nate closed the door and locked it before moving to stand beside Adam.

"Where is she?" Adam demanded.

"Where is who?" Carol returned.

"I don't have time to play games, Carol. Just tell me where she is."

"If you're talking about your whore, I have no idea where she is," she sneered.

Adam made a move toward her and Nate grabbed his arm to hold him back.

"Carol, we already know you were with Andrea out in the woods," Nate said quietly. "So, why don't you just tell us where she is and we'll leave."

"I don't know what you're talking about," she still insisted.

Nate reached in his pants pocket and pulled out the diamond earring. "I believe this belongs to you," he said. Carol paled slightly and shook her head. "We found it next to the edge of the cliff, so we know you were there."

A look of sheer hatred clouded her features as she made a grab for the earring. Nate snatched his hand back and put the earring back in his pocket.

"It only proves that I was there at some point, not that I had anything to do with her falling off the edge of the cliff."

"She fell off the cliff?" Adam whispered in horror.

"We were arguing and somehow she got too close to the edge. Next thing I knew, she was falling. I tried to grab her, but couldn't reach her," she lied.

"We searched the bottom of the cliff, Carol. Andrea wasn't there," Nate said, his voice deadly quiet.

Carol's eyes rounded in surprise. "But I saw her lying there on the ledge!" she cried.

Adam's hands clenched at his sides. "Why didn't you tell us when Nate dragged you into the house?"

"I was frightened! I knew you wouldn't believe me if I told you she accidentally fell!"

"I don't believe you now," Adam whispered dangerously. "I believe you kidnapped her."

"Why would I kidnap her?" she cried.

"Because you wanted her out of my life and you wanted me to believe that she just left on her own. But Andrea wouldn't do that because she knows how much I love her."

"You're lying," she whispered. "You can't love her, you love me."

Adam laughed harshly. "Good God, woman! You actually think I could love someone like you?"

"Adam, be careful," Nate warned at the look in Carol's eyes.

But Adam didn't heed Nate's warning as he continued. "The only thing you're good for is a roll in the sack. No decent man in his right mind would want you for anything else."

"You son of a bitch!" Carol screamed as she lunged at him.

Adam grabbed both of her wrists and turned her around, forcing her arms behind her back. "Now, you're going to tell me what you did with Andrea," he threatened.

Carol cried out as he tightened his grip on her. "I swear, Adam, she fell off the cliff and when I left, she was still there!"

Adam shoved her away and she fell to the floor. She stood up, glaring at him as she rubbed her wrists.

"Why?" she whispered. "After everything I've done for you, why can't you love me?"

"What have you done, Carol?" Nate, who had stood by and watched silently, asked quietly.

"I've loved you for so long. I've been there for you whenever you needed me." Her voice was low and her eyes were glazed as she continued. "I thought that when we got rid of Amanda, we would finally be together, that we would be married. Then this *woman* shows up and you ignore me and I see all my plans unraveling."

She focused her gaze on Nate. "I thought you would take care of Amanda for me, but you didn't. And you obviously couldn't take care of Andrea either," she sneered.

"Did you get someone else to help you?" Nate asked quietly.

Carol frowned as if she didn't understand the question.

"Amanda was thrown from her horse," Adam said, still concentrating on her statement about her getting rid of Amanda.

"Yes, she was. And Andrea fell off the cliff," she said, seeming confused.

Adam's whole body became rigid at the implication of her words. "You killed Amanda?" he asked quietly.

"I'm tired," she said sighing, as she sat down on the sofa.

Nate walked over and picked up the telephone.

"What are you doing?" Adam asked him.

"I'm calling the police now," Nate replied. At Adam's frown, he added, "Look, she all but admitted she had something to do with both Amanda's death and Andrea's disappearance. We have no choice but to bring in the police."

Adam looked down at Carol and sighed wearily. "I suppose you're right," he agreed. "But she still hasn't told us where Andrea is."

"I told you she was there when I left," Carol said quietly.

"The police are on their way," Nate said, after hanging up the telephone. "They want us to wait and answer some questions."

Adam shook his head as he sat down across from Carol. Her eyes were closed but Adam saw a tear slip from the corner of one eye. He knew he should feel sorry for her, but couldn't bring forth that emotion. She'd somehow had something to do with Amanda's death and Andrea's disappearance. All he could feel for her right now was hatred and disgust.

"I'm sorry I didn't believe you Nate," Adam said quietly.

Nate shrugged. "You had no reason to believe anything I told you." He saw the pain in Adam's eyes and said, "We'll find her."

Adam nodded, but didn't respond.

The police arrived and after what seemed like hours of questions and answers, they were told that both of them would have to come down to the station and give their statements to detectives. They watched as Carol

Judy Hinson

was taken away, never speaking another word to either of them.

"So, what do we do now, big brother?" Nate asked, as he sat down next to Adam.

"Do you think Carol was telling the truth about Andrea still being there when she left?" Adam asked quietly.

Nate sighed. "She sure thought she was telling the truth. Why?"

"Because if Andrea had fallen that distance, then the fall surely would have killed her."

"Most likely," Nate agreed.

"Then, where's her body?"

"I don't know."

"You read the newspaper articles. They said Andrea's body had never been recovered."

"You think she's back in her time, don't you?" Nate whispered.

"If Carol was telling the truth, then that's the only explanation." He stood and headed for the door. "Let's go."

"Where are we going now?" Nate asked, as he followed him.

"After we go to the police station, we're going back to have another look."

Chapter 21

*A*dam paced back and forth as he and Nate waited for Detective Logan to finish his interrogation with Carol. It seemed like hours since they had left Carol's apartment and he felt they were wasting valuable time in which to search for Andrea.

"Adam, will you please sit down? You're giving me a headache," Nate said.

"What the hell is taking so long?" Adam returned. Before Nate could respond, Detective Logan came out of the interrogation room.

"Well, did she tell you where Andrea is?" Nate asked as he stood.

"She said she knows nothing about Ms. Marsh's disappearance," Detective Logan replied.

"She's lying," Adam grated harshly.

"She admitted that she and Ms. Marsh had words, but she said that when she left, Ms. Marsh was fine."

"Then it was her partner. He has her," Nate told him.

"What partner?" Detective Logan asked, narrowing his eyes at Nate. "You never said anything about another person being involved in this."

"His name is Mike Stanton," Nate said.

"Mike Stanton?" Adam asked, shock registering on his face.

"Yea," Nate replied.

"I don't understand," Adam said. "Mike left town years ago. Why would he have anything to do with this?"

"I followed Carol to a bar one night and saw her meet with him. I couldn't hear what they were saying, but I did see Carol hand him an envelope and I'd bet my life that it was a payoff."

"Why didn't you tell me this before?" Adam asked.

"I tried to, but you didn't want to hear it!" Nate snapped.

"Who is this Stanton?" Detective Logan intervened.

Adam explained what had taken place between him and Mike years ago. "He swore he would have his revenge on me one day," he finished.

Logan shook his head. "Guys, without any evidence or solid proof that Ms. Masters had anything to do with Ms. Marsh's disappearance, my hands are tied."

"I just told you I saw Carol and Stanton together!" Nate cried.

"That doesn't mean they were plotting anything. They could have been two friends out for a drink."

"So, you're letting her go?" Adam asked quietly.

"I don't have any choice," Logan replied. "Get me proof that she had anything to do with this and I guarantee she'll be put away for a long time."

"What about her confession to us?" Nate inquired angrily.

"She said she never admitted anything to you two."

"Her word against ours," Nate sneered.

"She said you two frightened her and she said what she thought you wanted to hear."

"Let's go," Adam told Nate. "We're wasting time here."

At that moment, Carol walked out of the interrogation room. When Adam walked past her, she whispered, "I'm really sorry you think I had anything to do with this, Adam."

Adam turned stormy eyes on her. "If I find out that you and Mike had anything at all to do with Andrea's disappearance, you'll both wish you were dead."

Carol's eyes rounded in shock, but she never uttered a word as she watched her dream walk away.

***

Adam was standing at the edge of the cliff, gazing down, his whole body tense. He could feel her presence! He knew it was crazy, but he could sense her calling to him.

"Adam, we've searched this whole area a hundred times. Just what is it you're looking for?" Nate asked.

"I can feel her, Nate," he whispered. "That means there has to be a time portal around here somewhere."

"What?"

He turned around and looked at Nate. "Don't you see? When Andrea arrived here, it was in this area and if she went over the cliff, it has to be in this same area."

"Well, if there is a time portal around here, why haven't we found it?" Nate asked.

"I don't know!" Adam replied, frustrated. "But it's here, I just know it."

"Suppose there is a time portal here. Do you think you're just going to walk through it and get Andrea and bring her back?" Nate wanted to know.

"If I can figure out a way to do it, yes."

They rode back to the house and Adam went into the kitchen and put on a pot of coffee.

Nate stuck his head in the door and said, "I'm going on the Internet to see if I can find anything," and went to the library.

Adam entered the library a short time later with two cups of coffee. He sat one on the desk beside Nate.

Nate turned from the computer. "You know how much stuff there is on this subject? I mean some of it's weird, but some of its real science. Ever heard of the Philadelphia Experiment?"

Adam nodded and joined Nate at the desk as he continued.

"This dates back to the 1940's when radar invisibility was being researched. The USS Eldridge was stationed in the Philadelphia Naval Yard and involved in a test called the Philadelphia Experiment. The object was to make the ship undetectable to radar and while that was achieved, it had some pretty nasty results for the crewmembers. It was a catastrophe. Those who survived were discharged as mentally unfit or otherwise discredited and the whole affair was covered up."

"I remember hearing about that," Adam said quietly.

"Here's one that goes from time travel and the Pythagorean Theorem into Einstein. They jump straight into Einstein's Theory of Relativity which states neither time, nor length, nor even mass remain constant additive quantities when approaching the speed of light."

"The time portal has to be in that area," Adam said.

"So, you're going to try and go after her?" Nate asked.

"I have to."

"So, when do we leave?"

Adam frowned. "I need you here, in case something happens to me." Nate started to protest, but Adam held up hand. "I mean it, Nate. Sara and Daniel will need you if I don't come back."

"All right, I'll stay," he agreed grudgingly. "But nothing's going to happen to you. You will find Andrea and the two of you will return unharmed."

Adam grinned at his brother. "Damn right." He got up and headed for the stairs.

"Where are you going?" Nate asked.

"I have to go up and explain to Sara what has happened to Andrea," he replied.

"She loves Andrea very much," Nate said.

"Yes she does and I have to assure her that I will bring Andrea back safely."

Adam knocked softly on Sara's door and she bade him to enter. When he went in, he found Sara sitting at her desk.

"Doing your homework?" he asked.

She shook her head. "Writing in my diary," she replied.

"Sara, there's something I need to tell you," he said quietly. Sara frowned slightly as he continued. "Andrea has disappeared."

"What do you mean she's disappeared?"

"She went riding this morning and never returned."

"Do you think someone kidnapped her?"

"I did at first, but not now."

"What do you think happened to her?"

"I think she went home."

"Back in time?" Sara asked, shocked.

"Yes, that's what your Uncle Nate and I believe."

"How?"

He didn't want to tell her about Carol's involvement, so he made up a story. "I think that when she went riding this morning, she got too close to the cliff. Something must have spooked Max and she was thrown off, and must have went over the cliff."

"You think she went back to her time. That makes sense," she said. "What are you going to do?"

"Nate and I are discussing that now, trying to decide what to do."

"Is there any way she can come back?" she asked, tears beginning to form in her eyes.

"I don't know," he whispered. He gathered her in his arms and held her while she cried.

"What will happen to her and the baby if she doesn't come back?" she asked.

"I'm sure her father will take good care of her," he replied.

"But, if she stays there, she will have to marry Nathan," Sara said.

"I'm doing everything I can do try to get her back, Sara," he assured her. He kissed her on the forehead.

"Bring her home safe, daddy," she whispered.

Chapter 22

That evening, Andrea tried to find a plausible reason not to join her father and Nathan for dinner. She knew she had to face Nathan at some point, but wasn't sure how to answer his questions without giving her secret away.

Unable to avoid the confrontation she knew would come; she walked into the dining room. Both men rose from the table at her entrance and Nathan pulled out her chair for her.

"I'm glad to see you're feeling better," he said. "Your father tells me that you still don't remember what happened to you."

She glanced at her father sitting at the end of the table. "No, I don't."

"I'm sure it will come to you in time."

"I'm sure," she murmured.

Mattie came in and began serving dinner. Jonathan started the conversation by telling Andrea about the sale of the horses he had taken into Savannah and which ones he would take next week.

Nathan became annoyed with the conversation and interrupted. Looking at Andrea, he said, "Since you have returned home safely, I've spoken with Father Neely and he has agreed to perform our wedding ceremony as previously planned."

"I'm sorry Nathan, but I cannot marry you," she said quietly.

"Nonsense, it's all been arranged."

"I will not marry you," she told him firmly.

"You don't have a choice and I think you know why," he said coldly.

"Why do you want to marry me, Nathan? I know you don't love me and you know I don't love you, so why?"

"We will learn to love each other," he said matter-of-factly.

Andrea shook her head. "I will not marry a man I do not love," she said quietly.

"As I said, you don't have a choice," he reminded her.

"Ah, but she does," Jonathan interjected quietly. "I will not force Andrea into a marriage she does not want."

"We had a deal," Nathan said angrily.

"You made that deal with a man who had been drinking too much and was grieving," Andrea said in her father's defense.

"It doesn't matter," Jonathan said, giving his daughter a brief smile. "The deal is off."

"We had a deal, old man, and you will keep your end of it," Nathan growled as he pushed away from the table. He glared at Andrea then turned and left the room.

"I'm sorry, father," Andrea said quietly.

Jonathan waved his hand in the air. "You have nothing to be sorry for. I'm the one who sat down at the gaming table with him. If I had not done that, this would not have happened."

"But then I would never have met Adam and would not be carrying his child if you had not," she reminded him softly. A pained expression crossed his features. "It will be all right, I promise you," she told him.

"If you say so," Jonathan mumbled.

***

"You're going to do what?!" Nate asked in shock.

Adam grinned. "I'm going to jump out of a plane," he replied calmly.

"Jump out of a plane over the cliff and *hope* you pass through a time portal before you fall to your death? Have I got this right?"

"It's the only way I can do this."

"It's dangerous, Adam."

"There's no other way!" Adam snapped.

"What if it doesn't work?"

"It's going to work," Adam replied determinedly.

Nate sighed, knowing Adam had made up his mind. "When are you going to do this crazy stunt of yours?"

"Tomorrow morning."

"That soon?"

"I don't know how much time has passed in her world in the past three days. I can't take the chance of her marrying Nathan and him being the father of my child."

"I hadn't thought about that," Nate said. "Where are you going to get a plane from?"

"Joe said I could use his crop duster," he replied. Joe was the owner of the farm a mile down the road from them. "You're going to fly it."

"I was afraid you were going to say that," Nate said dryly. "I suppose you've already figured out how the two of you are going to get back," he said.

Adam smiled wryly. "Not entirely," he admitted. "I'm going to take an extra parachute for Andrea and we're going to jump off the cliff and pray we pass through the time portal."

"Jesus, Adam, you're crazy!" Nate whispered.

"I don't know of any other way, Nate," Adam said quietly.

"What if Andrea doesn't want to come back? What if seeing her father again has made her realize that she doesn't belong here? What will you do then?"

"She'll come back," he said determinedly. "We'll meet at the stables at six o'clock tomorrow morning and then head over to Joe's," Adam told him. "Now, why don't we sit down and try to figure all this out and make sure our calculations are correct," he suggested.

***

That night, Adam went into Sara's room and explained what he was going to do.

"Isn't this dangerous, daddy?" she asked, concern evident in her voice when Adam told her that he was going to go get Andrea.

"I have to do this, Sara, if we have any chance of ever seeing Andrea again," he told her quietly.

"What if she doesn't want to come back?" she asked worriedly.

"Why wouldn't she want to come back?" Adam asked in return. "She has made a new life here with us and I believe she is trying to find a way to get back to us just as I am finding a way to get to her."

Tears gathered in her eyes as she hugged him. "Please be careful and both of you come home safely."

He kissed her on the forehead. "I promise. Andrea and I will be home before you know it."

***

The next morning, Nate met Adam as planned. After Nate had left the day before, Adam had gone into town and purchased the equipment he would need.

As Nate took off, he glanced back at Adam who was strapping his parachute on. "You're crazy, you know that," he yelled.

Laughing, Adam nodded. "Crazy in love!" He yelled back.

He moved closer to the door as the cliff came into view.

"Ready?" Nate yelled.

"Ready," Adam yelled back. If he faced death, he would do it for Andrea. And, in that moment, in a startling flash of clarity, he knew that the love in his heart was far stronger than anything.

"Go!" Nate wiped a tear from the corner of his eyes. "You better come back, you son of a bitch," he whispered.

Adam jumped and his body instinctively curled into a fetal position. He began to float as he took hold of the straps. He could see the ground coming at him and looked up.

Earth: sky: earth: sky.

On and on it went as he tumbled and became disoriented. He closed his eyes against the dizzying sight as the wind stripped him of breath, and then something happened. A bright light flashed behind his closed lids and he thought for a moment that he had died, for he felt a frisson of heat saturate every cell of his body and infuse it with odd energy. Then he seemed to enter a peaceful state, a place where he heard himself saying to arch his back.

Immediately, he straightened out and opened his eyes. Spread-eagled and falling, he knew he was not in his world.

His fingers touched the handle at his chest and he was shot straight up. Pulling the left one, he turned toward the edge of the cliff. He hit the ground hard, and was sure his ankles had broken with the impact as pain shot up his body and rammed into the top of his skull. Suddenly he was jerked backward and his legs crumpled under them. His back and head hit the ground.

He passed out.

Chapter 23

Andrea tiptoed down the stairs, grabbed her shawl from the hook by the front door and threw it around her shoulders. She went through the kitchen and slipped out the back door.

She breathed a sigh of relief as she closed the door. She walked around the stables and through the back so she wouldn't be seen if anyone happened to be looking out one of the front windows.

When she reached the outer edge of the woods, she glanced behind her to make sure no one had followed her. Satisfied that no one had, she sat down beneath an oak tree.

She wasn't sure what she was going to do. Nathan continued to insist that she marry him and no amount of arguing with him was changing his mind. But she wasn't going to do it. She would not sacrifice herself and her child by marrying a man she didn't love.

If she never saw Adam again, she would have a part of him that no one could take away from her.

Her thoughts were interrupted by a loud roar. Shading her eyes against the sun, she looked up and for a split second, thought she saw one of those airplanes Sara had told her about. But she knew that was impossible, she was in her time, not Sara's.

Suddenly, the roar seemed to rock the ground beneath her and she could see a flash of light and something falling from the sky.

She stood transfixed as she watched whatever it was hit the ground hard. Shaken, she moved hesitantly toward the bundle lying on the ground.

Terror raced through her when she was close enough to realize that it was a man lying there.

"Oh my God!" she breathed when she realize who it was. "Adam…" She breathed his name as she bent down and touched his jaw. "Wake up." Fear and confusion filled her as she tried to undo the thick knot around him.

"Adam!" Desperate, she again called out his name as she scrambled to untangle the last few slips of the knot. Finally free, she pulled the rope from around his shoulders and back and started slapping Adam's cheeks.

"Wake up. You can't be dead." She laid her head against his chest and had to hold her breath in order to hear his heart.

It was pumping, and she felt his chest expand with his shallow breathing.

"Okay, wake up," she cried, and shook his shoulders. He moaned lightly and Andrea froze in mid shake, her eyes clouded by a film of tears. "Please, Adam…please wake up. That's right, you can do it. I'm here and I need you. You have to get up. Now, Adam…right now."

His eyelids fluttered once and he moaned louder.

"That's it. Come on. Wake up." She tapped his cheek lighter this time. "Adam…it's Andrea. *Wake up!*"

"All right," he mumbled. "Stop yelling."

Stunned for a moment, she stared at him and then broke into a soft smile. "You're okay. Thank God, you're okay. I thought you might be–" She stopped herself short with the thought and continued in a whisper. "What are you doing here? How did you get here?"

He opened his eyelids and blinked a few times as another painful moan escaped his lips.

"Andrea," he murmured.

"It's me, Adam. How did you get here?"

"I jumped."

"You…jumped? Jumped from what?"

"From an airplane," he replied.

He was here. Joy surged through her body, replacing the shock.

He was here!

She looked down at the man before her and smiled.

"Adam…you're here," she whispered.

He simply nodded, as though even that was taking more effort than he wanted to expend.

He closed his eyes and she fell forward to hug him. Hearing his rush of breath leave his chest, she quickly sat up.

"You came for me," she whispered, tears in her eyes.

"You didn't think I would just let you disappear from my life, did you?"

She smiled through her tears and bent to softly kiss him.

She took the silk material and the bag he had with him and hid it behind some brush and returned to his side.

It took them some time to get him upright but she did and Andrea led him through the woods.

Thankfully, no one saw them as she took him to the front parlor and placed him on the sofa.

"How are you feeling?" she asked.

"I feel like my head is about to explode," he replied.

"I'll go get you some water."

She made to leave and he grabbed her wrist. "It's really you," he murmured.

She smiled. "It's really me."

She went and got a glass of water and lifted his head to help him drink. He took a long swallow and leaned back against the arm of the sofa.

"Adam, how did you do it? How did you travel through time?" she asked softly.

"I jumped out of an airplane and thankfully landed in the time portal."

"Landed in what?"

He moaned softly as he tried to sit up.

"We can talk about this later. You need to rest."

He closed his eyes and Andrea sat on the floor in front of him and watched him.

"I had to find you," he whispered.

"I'm glad you did," she said, smiling. "How did you know I had traveled back in time?"

"Nate was convinced that Carol had something to do with your disappearance, so we confronted her."

"She admitted she pushed me off the cliff?" Andrea asked, surprised.

"Not in so many words," he replied. "But she did admit that she was with you but told us you had fallen off the cliff."

"She lied, Adam. She pushed me off," Andrea said quietly.

"I know," he said. "When she said you were there when she left, the only conclusion I could come to was that when you fell, you went through the time portal."

"What is a time portal?" she asked.

"It's like a time machine where you can pass through the future to the present to the past."

"I don't understand," she said, frowning.

"It's really hard to explain. There's this energy field beyond the woods and when you fell off the cliff, you obviously passed through the time portal."

"How did you know that's where this time portal was?"

"I could feel your presence in that area and I could hear you calling me," he replied softly.

Her eyes clouded with tears. "I *was* calling for you. I was afraid I would never see you again."

Adam finally managed to sit up and pulling Andrea into his arms, brushed her lips with hers. "I was afraid I would never see you again, too," he whispered.

"What in the blue blazes is going on? Andrea, who is this man?"

Andrea groaned inwardly when she heard her father's voice. Turning to him, she smiled. "Father, I would like you to meet Adam. Adam, this is my father, Jonathan Marsh."

Andrea smiled at the shocked expression on her father's face at the sight of her leaning over Adam.

Adam managed to sit up as Jonathan came into the room. "I apologize for not being able to get up, but I am still somewhat disoriented from my trip."

"And, just how the hell did you get here?" Jonathan asked, staring unabashed at Adam.

"It's a long story, father," Andrea replied for Adam. "We will tell you all about it as soon as Adam is feeling better."

"I'm fine, Andrea," Adam assured her.

"Perhaps a cup of tea will help," Andrea suggested. "Father, would you please ask Mattie to make a pot of tea?"

"Huh? Oh, yes, yes." He left the room, shaking his head.

"I think we've shocked him," Andrea told Adam, smiling.

"You haven't told him about me?"

"I did, but I don't think he truly believed me until now," she replied.

Adam placed his hand on her stomach and looked at her inquiringly. "Are you all right?"

Andrea smiled softly. "The baby and I are fine."

"Good," he said quietly. "I was afraid the trip back would have an effect on you and him, or her."

"The only effect it had was the thought of never seeing you again," she whispered.

Jonathan returned and placed the tray down on the table. Andrea poured tea in one cup and handed it to Adam. "I know you don't really like tea, but it will help," she told him.

"It will probably help better if there was a spot of whiskey in it," Jonathan said as he went to the liquor cabinet and grabbing a bottle of whiskey, poured some in Adam's tea. Andrea frowned, but said nothing. Adam thanked Jonathan and took a sip.

Jonathan poured himself a glass of whiskey and sat down. "Feeling better?" he asked.

"Yes, thank you," Adam replied.

"Good. Now, will someone tell me what the hell is going on?"

"Father, please. Can't this wait until later?" Andrea asked.

"It's all right, Andrea." Adam said, taking her hand in his. "Where would you like me to start?" he asked Jonathan.

"Are you really from the future?" Jonathan asked.

Adam smiled. "Yes, I'm really from the future."

"Have you disappeared in your time as Andrea did here?"

"Not in the same manner. I found the time portal that Andrea had passed through and parachuted out of an airplane."

"You did what out of what?" Jonathan asked, horrified.

"I jumped out of an airplane."

"What the devil is an airplane?"

"We'll explain all that later, Father," Andrea said. She looked back at Adam and asked, "How did you know that the time portal was located near the cliff?"

"Nate and I calculated the distance from the bottom of the cliff where you had fallen and gauged that if I jumped over that area, I would most likely pass through the time portal."

"I didn't fall. I was pushed," Andrea reminded him.

"I know. Nate convinced me that Carol was out to hurt you and when confronted, she finally admitted it."

"Who is Nate?" Jonathan asked.

"Nate is Adam's younger brother," Andrea replied.

"So, Andrea's story is true, you really are descendants of Nathan." Jonathan said.

"Yes. Nathan is my great grandfather," Adam replied.

"How do you propose we get back?" Andrea asked Adam.

"Back? Surely you're not going back, Andrea?" Jonathan asked, surprised.

"Of course," she replied.

"You can't leave now." Jonathan gasped.

"My life is with Adam, Father," Andrea said quietly. Adam groaned softly, bringing her attention back to him. "I think you need to lie down and rest for a while," she suggested.

"I guess the fall I took was a lot worse than I thought," Adam said, grimacing.

Andrea helped him up and looked at her Father. "We'll talk about this later," she said quietly.

"Yes, we will," Jonathan reassured her.

Andrea placed Adam's arm around her shoulder and she led him from the room. They made their way up the stairs and Andrea opened the door to the room next to hers.

"I'm going to find Mattie and have her bring something for your head," she told him after she had gotten him into the bed.

"A couple of aspirin would be nice," Adam said, smiling.

"I'll be right back," she promised.

She went down the back stairs to the kitchen, sure she would find Mattie there. However, she wasn't in the kitchen. Shrugging, she went to the pantry and found an ice pack and filling it with water from the pitcher on the table, headed back up the stairs. She smiled when she opened the door and found Adam sleeping. She placed the ice pack on the table next to the bed and gently ran a finger down the side of his face. She couldn't believe he was really here. She had dreamed that he would come for her, but never thought he could actually do it.

She thought she would never see him again and would have to settle for having his child to keep his memory alive for her.

She softly kissed his forehead and pulled the covers over him. She hoped that he would feel better after some sleep.

She went back downstairs in search of her father. He was still sitting in the parlor where she had left him, a drink in his hand.

She stood in front of him, frowning. "I don't want you getting drunk until we've talked," she told him sternly.

He looked up at her. "This is the same drink I had when you left," he reassured her. "Now, will you explain to me what an airplane is, and what a time portal is?"

Andrea told him all she knew from what Sara had told her about airplanes, and relayed what Adam had told her about the time portal. "Now, maybe you can explain to me what you're doing with all that money in the safe in the study." she told him.

"How do you know about that?" he asked. "Never mind," he said when she frowned at him. "That is the money from the sale of the horses that I took to town. I haven't had time to put it in the bank yet."

She nodded as she knelt down on her knees and took his hand in hers. "Father, I have to go back with Adam. My life is with him, in the future."

"I won't lose you again, Andrea." he spoke quietly. "I almost went crazy when we couldn't find you. I thought I had lost you forever, just as I had lost your mother. I know I hurt you very much with my drinking and gambling and getting involved with Nathan. But, I promise you, I've changed and I will fight Nathan to keep him away from you." He frowned as a thought occurred to him. "How are you going to explain Adam to Nathan?" he asked.

"I don't have to explain anything to Nathan," she told him. "I am not pledged to him and owe him nothing."

"If you don't marry him, you know what he will do."

"I told you how everything will end, Father. If I stay and by some ungodly reason marry Nathan, it will change the future for Adam and his family. And I won't do that. I can't do that."

"Then, I'm going with you," he stated flatly.

"What?"

"You heard me. If you go back with Adam, I'm going back with you. I will not stay here without you."

"Father, you can't. If you go with me, it could change things."

"Like what?" he asked. "You said Nathan ends up with this house and that it is handed down through the generations. My staying here with Nathan is only because I couldn't be with you. If I go, he will still get this house and your Adam still inherits it."

"I think your father may have something there." Adam said from the doorway.

"Adam! What are you doing up? Are you all right?" she asked worriedly as she stood.

"I'm better," he replied, coming in and sitting down on the sofa across from Jonathan. He reached for Andrea's hand and pulled her down beside him.

"According to the newspaper articles we found, Nathan marries, lives in this house and it is handed down through the generations. The only mention of you, Jonathan, was that you lived here with Nathan and his family until your death. At a ripe old age, I might add."

"What are you getting at, Adam?" Andrea asked.

"I don't see how your father going with us will change anything. I don't think his being here now or in the future, has any bearing on my grandfather, father, or Nate and I being born. Jonathan was never mentioned as being a grandfather or uncle or any relation to my ancestors. So why not take him with us, if that's what he wants?"

"Is that what you truly want, Father?" Andrea asked quietly.

"I want to be wherever you are, Andrea," he replied.

"Then, it's settled," Adam said.

"Want to tell me just how you plan to get us back?" Jonathan asked.

Adam frowned slightly. "Nate and I discussed that and there's only one way we can do this."

"And how is that?" Jonathan asked.

"We jump off the cliff."

"What?!" Andrea gasped. "You can't be serious!"

"How will we know the exact place to jump and end up in this 'time portal'?" Jonathan asked.

"Nate and I figured that jumping and landing on the ledge below the cliff is where the time portal is."

"And if it isn't?" Andrea asked quietly.

"Nate and I went over and over this, Andrea. It's the only logical place it can be," he replied. "Carol said that when you went over the cliff, you landed on that ledge, that she saw you there."

"But, that's not where I found you, Adam," she said.

"But it was close to the same spot, right?"

"Well, yes, I guess it was."

"I think that the time portal is very large and covers that whole area. So if we jump off the cliff near the ledge, we will land right on or near the spot where you were found."

"I don't know, Adam," she said hesitantly. "We could all be killed if you're not sure."

He took her hands between his and looked directly in her eyes. "We don't have any other choice, Andrea. If we want to go home, we have to do this."

"What happens if only one of us makes it back? What if I am the only one that makes it? What will I tell your family?" she asks worriedly.

"That I love them and will always love them and that you will take care of them," he replied softly.

"I don't want to make it if you don't," she whispered, tears gathering in her eyes.

"You and your brother, the two of you thought this thing out and you're sure we can do it?" Jonathan asked.

"We did and I'm sure we can do it," Adam replied.

"Then, when do we do it?"

"The sooner the better," he replied. "I have no idea how long the time portal will remain open and don't want to take the chance of it closing on us before we get through it."

"Will you be up to doing it tomorrow?"

Adam smiled. "Yes, sir," he searched Andrea's face. "Are you ready to do this?"

"I guess so," she whispered. "I will go later and get your things that I hid behind the tree," she told him.

"There you are, Jonathan. Where is Andr… what is going on here? Who the hell are you?" Nathan demanded of Adam as he came into the room and found Andrea in his arms.

"Oh, God!" Andrea breathed. She felt Adam stiffen beside her as he turned to face his great grandfather.

Chapter 24

*N*ate found Sara staring out the living room window when he came downstairs the next morning.

"Sara honey, are you all right?"

"I'm worried about dad and Andrea," she replied.

"They're going to be okay," he assured her.

"How do you know that? How do you know if dad even made it to Andrea?" she asked bitterly. "I don't know why I'm even talking to you. I'm still mad at you," she added coldly.

"Because of your mother," Nate said quietly.

"If you hadn't come between her and dad, she'd still be alive."

"You know what happened?" he asked, surprised.

"Of course, I'm not stupid." she replied. "I know you and mom were having an affair and that she wanted to leave dad to be with you."

Nate sat down in the chair opposite her by the window. "Your mother and I fell in love, Sara," he said quietly. "We didn't plan it. It just happened. And if you want to hate me for that, then you'll just have to hate me. I won't apologize for loving your mother."

She looked at him with tears in her eyes. "But if you and mom hadn't fallen in love, she and dad wouldn't have been fighting that day and she wouldn't have fallen off her horse."

"It was an accident, Sara," he said quietly. "If it hadn't of been that day, it could have been another day. When it's your time to go, Sara, there's nothing anyone can do to prevent it." He knew he was lying to her, but refused to upset her even more by telling her Carol's involvement in Amanda's accident.

"I'm afraid I'm going to lose dad now! I'm afraid that he and Andrea will never return!" she cried.

"They will return!" he said roughly. "Your father will find Andrea and bring her home!"

"You promise?" she whispered brokenly.

"I promise," he whispered, taking her in his arms and holding her tightly.

God, he hoped he was right and that Sara wouldn't lose another parent because of him.

***

"This isn't your house yet, Nathan, so I would appreciate you not barging in without being announced," Jonathan said angrily.

Nathan ignored Jonathan as he glared at Adam. "Your familiarity with my fiancée better mean you're a relative," he said coldly.

"Sort of," Adam said, smiling slightly.

"Oh, Nathan," Andrea sighed heavily. "I'm not your fiancée and who Adam is certainly is none of your business."

Adam squeezed her hand and stood. "I'm a distant cousin of Andrea's mother and when I heard of her death, I came as soon as I could."

"Claudia has been dead for over three years," Nathan stated flatly.

"I was abroad and didn't receive the news until several months ago."

"And just how long are you planning on staying?"

"Not long," he replied, smiling. "I just came to pay my respects and will try to leave tomorrow."

"Father, didn't you say Mattie was making a special dinner for our guest and that it would be ready soon?" Andrea asked, abruptly changing the subject.

"Yes, I did," he replied.

"Then, I suggest we get cleaned up for dinner," Andrea said, taking Adam's hand. She looked at Nathan and smiled. "You don't mind if we have a family dinner alone, do you? I haven't seen Adam in years and we have a lot of catching up to do."

"Of course," Nathan replied stiffly. "But, tomorrow we need to sit down and go over our wedding plans."

"You two are getting married?" Adam asked with feigned surprise.

"Yes, very soon," Nathan replied.

"Well, congratulations," Adam said, extending his hand. Nathan took the hand Adam offered and shook it quickly.

"Why don't we see what happens tomorrow, then maybe we'll discuss the wedding plans," Andrea suggested.

The three of them walked Nathan to the door and after closing it, Jonathan locked it.

"He sure doesn't look as fierce in person as I thought he would," Adam commented.

"Nathan's really not a bad person," Jonathan said quietly.

"He's a bully and enjoys hurting people," Andrea said.

"He just comes off that way," Jonathan said in Nathan's defense.

"I don't want to talk about Nathan," Andrea said. "I'm going to go get Adam's things, then go upstairs to freshen up and will meet you two in the dining room." She reached up and kissed Adam lightly on the lips, then kissed her father on the cheek.

***

Up in her room, she washed her face and hands in the fresh bowl of water Mattie had left and changed her clothes. When she went back downstairs, Adam and her father were already seated at the dining room table.

Adam stood and pulled out the chair next to her. A moment later, Mattie came in with the first course and after dipping a spoon of soup in each bowl, left the room.

"Father, I need to let Saralyn know what's going on," Andrea said.

"You can't do that, Andrea," Adam said.

"Why not?"

"You can't do anything that could possibly change the future," he replied.

"But she needs to know that I'm safe," Andrea argued.

"If you contact her now, she may never come back here and will never marry Nathan."

"She will be devastated when she sees that I never return."

"Nathan consoles her in her grief, remember?"

Andrea sighed. "You're right."

She looked at her father. "What about Mattie?" Andrea asked quietly.

"What about her?" he returned.

"We can't just leave her here with Nathan."

Jonathan smiled. "I've already spoken to Mattie after our discussion earlier. I explained things to her, which I don't think she really understood, and told her that Nathan would be living in this house. She refused to stay here once he moved in, so she is going to stay with her sister over in Marion County. I will give her the money from the sale of the horses. It is enough to tide her over for a long time. Is that satisfactory with you?"

"But, what will she think when we leave the house tomorrow and don't return?"

"She won't be here, Andrea. She is leaving tonight, so she won't know what we are doing."

"Thank you, Father," Andrea said.

They ate their soup in silence and after Mattie removed the bowls and brought in the main course, Andrea broached the subject of their travel arrangements.

"Adam, since we don't have any of those parachutes that you spoke of, what will Father and I use?"

"Your Father and I were discussing that while you were upstairs. I brought an extra one with me for you, but since I didn't know your father would be coming with us, I didn't bring an extra one. However, he told me that you have bolts of silk up in the attic that you use to make dresses. That's what we'll make another parachute out of."

"And we're going to use the harnesses from the stables as pull cords to release the silk," Jonathan said.

"And you know how to do this?" she asked Adam.

"Yes," he replied, smiling. He reached over and took her hand. "It will work, Andrea, I promise." She nodded, but made no response.

Jonathan asked Adam a question and he responded, and then asked another. Andrea ate her meal in silence as she listened to their conversation.

After the meal was finished, Adam and Jonathan went up to the attic and gathered all the silk Andrea had stored there, then the two of them went out to the stables and began gathering up all the harnesses.

Andrea walked into the kitchen and quietly stood watching Mattie placing the food in the ice chest.

Tears came to her eyes at the thought of never seeing her again.

"Is you okay, baby?" Mattie asked when she saw the tears in Andrea's eyes.

"I was just thinking about all the years we've been together," Andrea replied.

Mattie smiled. "You took my heart the minute I laid eyes on you," she said. "I knew right then you'd be a fighter and would get what you wanted outta this old world."

"I missed you while I was gone, but I'm going to miss you even more knowing I'll never see you again."

"We'll sees each other again, baby. I ain't got no doubt bout that," Mattie assured her. She gathered Andrea in her arms and hugged her. "Don't know exactly what's going on, but I sense that young man out there with yor daddy is a good man and will take care of you."

"I love him very much," Andrea whispered.

She shook her head and smiled. "I's can tell that."

"Will you be all right with your sister?"

"She been begging me to come live with her since her husband died. Ain't no way I's staying here with that Mr. Rivers."

Andrea smiled through her tears. "I love you Mattie."

"I loves you too, baby," she replied. "Now, go help yor daddy and yor man get ready to leave tomorrow."

"Thank you for being here for me," Andrea whispered.

"You's take care of yorself and that baby and don't worry about me, I'll be just fine," she said as she turned back to her task.

Andrea wiped the tears from her eyes and went out to the stables. Adam and her father were cutting holes in the silk fabric and running the harness cords through them. She asked what she could do to help and Adam told her she could tear up some more silk.

They worked throughout the night and just before daybreak, had finished.

Adam suggested they get some rest and that at noon, they would gather everything and go to the cliff.

"Will you lie with me?" Andrea asked when they reached her bedroom door.

"What about your father?"

She shrugged her shoulders. "I need for you to hold me," she whispered.

He followed her in and closed the door. They laid down on the bed and Adam gathered her in his arms. "I love you," he whispered against her hair.

"I love you too," she said.

"By this time tomorrow, we'll be home with Sara and Daniel," he told her.

"I've missed them."

"They've missed you, too. Even Nate has missed you."

She laughed softly. "I think Nate and I are going to be very good friends," she yawned and closed her eyes.

Adam, however, couldn't close his eyes. He didn't want Andrea or Jonathan to know, but he was worried. He knew that he and Nate were right about the time portal, but it still worried him that their calculations might be off just a little. And, if that were the case, one or all three of them could die.

He said a silent prayer as he pulled Andrea closer to him.

***

"Now, remember, pull that flap when I tell you to," Adam told them, pointing to the makeshift belt he'd had to invent to release the cord on Jonathan's. It was made out of belt buckles and the metal from the harnesses.

"But, what if it doesn't work?" Andrea asked worriedly.

"It will," Adam assured her. "Jonathan, is yours secure?"

"All secure," Jonathan replied.

"The wind is blowing pretty hard, Adam," Andrea commented.

"That's a good thing."

"But won't it steer us off course?"

"Not if you use the cords the way I told you to, to control your direction."

"Adam, I'm scared," she whispered.

"Me too," he whispered back. "Just hold onto my hand and don't let go, no matter what happens." She nodded her head. "Jonathan, are you ready?" Adam asked.

"Ready as I'll ever be," Jonathan replied.

"The next gust of wind and we go," he told them.

Within moments, another gust of wind cut across the field. "One, two, three!" Adam yelled and they began to run.

Andrea began to panic as the edge of the cliff came nearer. She made to stop and Adam shook his head furiously.

Crossing herself, she jumped when Adam jumped and screamed as she went flying through the air.

Epilogue

"*I* owe you an apology," Nate said, as he sat down in the rocker next to Andrea.

"For what?" Andrea asked.

"For not protecting you more from Carol."

"You warned me about her, Nate. It wasn't your responsibility to protect me from her."

"No, it was mine," Adam said as he came out on the porch and joined them. "Nate told me time after time about how dangerous she was, but I wouldn't listen."

"Neither one of you could have known that she was capable of hurting anyone. She had been your friend for a very long time," Andrea said quietly.

"But, I saw the warning signs," Nate said.

"What do you suppose happened to her?" Andrea asked.

"If she was smart, she packed up and left town," Nate replied.

"I had the superintendent open her apartment when I went over there the other day. It was clean. Not a trace of Carol anywhere," Adam told them.

"I spoke with Detective Logan," Nate said. "He found Stanton in Atlanta."

"Did he admit to anything?" Adam asked.

Nate shook his head. "Said he never heard of Carol Masters," he replied. "And with no proof, of course, Detective Logan couldn't charge him with anything."

"Then I guess everything turned out the way it was supposed to," Andrea said quietly.

Several days after their return, Adam had went to the library to check the old newspaper clippings to see if they had changed history. He found everything to be as it should be.

"How do you suppose Nathan reacted when he went to Briarcliff the next morning and found the house empty?" Adam asked.

Andrea smiled sheepishly. "I left him a note."

"What did you tell him?" Adam asked, raising an eyebrow.

"I told him it would never work between us and that father and I were going abroad with you and I hoped one day he would understand and forgive me."

"He obviously did," Nate said dryly, waving a hand around the house.

Andrea looked out across the front yard where her father had her son, Steven, on a blanket on the ground as they watched Sara and Daniel play a game of softball.

"I'd say everything turned out just right," Adam said as he pulled Andrea to her feet and wrapped her in his arms.

"Do you think the time portal is still there?" Nate asked quietly.

"I don't think we'll ever know," Adam replied.

"I don't think I want to know," Andrea said softly. Her travel back to the future was one experience she would never want to try again.

She had been the first one to land and had been thankful that she and her baby were unharmed. She had begun to panic when Adam and her father had not returned when she had. She had been afraid that they would not return and she would be here alone.

She had been relieved when both of them appeared and neither one of them were harmed either.

Her reunion with Sara had been a tearful one and she had vowed to never let Andrea out of her sight again.

"Any regrets?" he asked Andrea.

"None," she replied, brushing his lips with hers.

Adam wrapped his arms around her tighter as the kiss deepened, oblivious to anyone or anything around them.

"Do you two mind?" Nate growled.

Andrea chuckled softly as she pulled out of Adam's embrace.

"Dad!" Sara called. "Will you and Uncle Nate come play with us?"

"Sure, why not," Nate mumbled as he got up and walked out to where the kids were playing.

"I think we need to find a nice girl for Nate," Andrea commented.

"That's going to be hard, unless we go back in time and find someone like you," he said.

"Why do you say that?" she inquired.

"Because I guarantee you that no one like you exists in this time," he replied.

"Oh, Adam," she laughed softly, shaking her head.

"You coming or not?" Nate demanded of Adam.

"Be right there," Adam replied. He bent down and gave Andrea another long kiss. "I love you," he whispered.

"I love you too," she whispered back.

She watched as Adam ran down the steps to join Nate and the children, her heart still filled with all the love she felt for him.

It was an infinite love that would outshine all dimensions of time; a timeless love.

About the Author

Photograph By: Jaime Warren

Judy Hinson lives in Middle Georgia with her husband Art, her daughter Jaime, son-in-law Mac, her two granddaughters, Hailey and Jillian, and her mother and brother.

Judy's Website
Grandpas Bird Houses.com

L & L Publishers

"A beautifully written story of love, intrigue, mystery and suspense put together. It captivates the reader in the first few paragraphs and holds their attention. I found I could not wait to see what was going to happen to Andrea next. This suspense-filled romance novel keeps you reading it until you are finished, and can turn anyone into a compulsive reader. I have read many romance novels since I was a young lady and find this novel to be one of many that I hope to read more of from this author."

–Yvette Morin
Avid Romance Reader

"This book is as good as it gets. One of those books that is hard to put down. The story just carries you away. A really enjoyable read about a love that was truly timeless. A romance so powerful, that it transcended time."

–Dianna Kume
Itty Bitty Blessings.com

"Timeless Love is destined to become a favorite of romance and non-romance readers alike and Judy Hinson is on her way to becoming one of the top romance authors of our time. The story is skillfully written and it transports the reader between 1889 and 2003 with ease. The plot and the characters are so well developed that they come alive and captivate the reader. It is a love story filled with family strife, conflict, romance and most importantly timeless love. This book is a must-read and will be enjoyed for years to come."

–Stephanie D. Burton
Attorney

"I found it so interesting that I couldn't pull away from it, and so I had to stay up all night with a flashlight at my cottage reading it."

–Alanna Roberts
Teenage daughter of Manager Kevin Roberts
Kallen Homes.ca

"This book really was captivating. I couldn't put it down. I was only sorry that I had to stop and go to work this afternoon. I couldn't wait to get home to finish it. And I did finish it, right after work...all in one day. Great story line and one couldn't help but wonder "Could it really happen???""

–Denise Woodman
Woody's Trim

"Timeless Love is a must-read romance! I fell in love with Judy Hinson's well-developed, captivating characters and was compelled to stay up in to the wee hours to finish this enthralling love story. I felt transported back in time myself! It was absolutely enchanting from cover to cover."

–Shannon Connolly
Bonny Babies.com

"I have been daydreaming about my lost love since I finished the book. It was amazing how the author could provoke such strong emotions in me--ones we can all relate to as women. Thanks for the chance to escape. A truly awesome read."

–Donna Bliss
My Miracle Baby.com

"When I picked up Timeless Love, I never expected to be so quickly drawn into a love story that would leave me wanting to know more. It was so easy to get caught up in these lives-I was tearful one minute then cheering the next as the story progressed. The romance blended so well with a family struggling to regain its footing that you couldn't help but care for these characters and hope for a happy ending. I thoroughly enjoyed reading Timeless Love and would recommend it for all romance readers out there."

–Kathryn Peddle
Buddy Blankies.com

"A truly mesmerizing love story, filled with romance and intrigue...one that you will find yourself being unable to put down until the last page and wanting to read all over again."

–Shar Croy
Lullaby-Creations.com

"It was so refreshing to read such a beautiful love story by Judy Hinson. I truly came to know each character and fell in love over and over again. It was a book I had to keep reading till the very last page."

–Beckie McCuen
Baby Scrubs.com

"Captivating from page one. The intriguing and spellbinding pages kept me turning and reading to see what happened next. I give it two thumbs up!"

–Lori Ramsey
Author of 'Baby in Me'
Tootlebug.com

"The most enchanting romance novel...proving without a shadow of doubt that love travels through the ages...and that true love is timeless."

—Georgene Freedman
Heartbeat Designs.com

Timeless Love

Judy Hinson

Printed in the United States
73678LV00001B/41

9 780973 553468